Wolfsong Beloved
A Novel

Drew John Ladd

For Tyre
&
The rest of Us

Prelude: Just A Boy

I was awakened by insistent rapping of metal on wood, a knock upon on our door. Before I'd properly opened my eyes, father was on his feet and signaling to me to lie down and stay quiet. I watched him gather a robe about himself before heading off to answer, sword in hand.

He was dragged outside almost immediately after opening the door. I leapt from my bed and rushed toward him, grabbing my sword along the way.

The men were large and armed, all six carrying the stink of sickness. One of them lay near the front door, with a great slash through his chest armor, his hands frozen into supple claws, his eyes locked in permanent surprise. The other five had managed to subdue father.

They had him pinned to an elm tree, a sword run through his shoulder. One of the men held a dagger with which he meant to cut his throat. My father cried out like a wounded animal.

"Run, boy! I'm already dead! You must -"

The largest of the men struck my father hard enough to render him unconscious.

I couldn't cry out. I couldn't breathe. My vision blurred with tears. After years of running, it seemed it would end with my father being murdered before my eyes. "No!", my heart cried.

"No," I spoke aloud. Sword in hand, I rushed to meet them.

They seemed to take no notice of me until the moment I was in striking distance and, even then, the first of them didn't take me seriously. He taunted me on my approach, bracing for me with a weak defensive stance, his full weight resting on his front leg, his sword sheathed. Before the last taunt fell from his lips, I had taken his left arm above the elbow and buried my sword in his belly to the hilt. He looked from his gushing limb to me and back in disbelief.

"Just... a boy", he gurgled and fell to his knees. I took his head.

Four men remained.

Two of them drew their swords and approached me. One, perhaps thinking he was clever, circled around, hoping to flank me. I let him.

The first rushed and began overwhelming me with a volley of heavy blows, each one sending violent reports of pain up my arms. My hands began to hurt. I knew it wouldn't be long before my shoulders gave out. "Four more men", I thought, and steeled myself.

The man in front of me drew back for another heavy blow just as the man behind me made his move. At the last possible moment, I pivoted and dropped to my knees. The man to my rear swung his sword for my head, and missed. With all my strength, I thrust my sword upward into the shelf of his chin. He made a face as if he were going to cry out but didn't. Instead, he stood there. Stunned. Dying.

I heard the whisper of another sword coming for my head and rolled out of the way. I was not able to retrieve my sword.

Three men remained.

The two who had remained with my father now drew their swords and came for me.

One of the men struck with a downward blow, meaning to cleave me in half. I stepped into and under his blow, catching him by the wrists and tossing him over my hip, disarming him in the process. I planted his own sword into his face. His hands flew to his face clawed at the blade. But only for a moment. Then he was still.

Two men remained.

One of the men snarled and lunged at me. I side-stepped the tip of his sword, only to step on the handle of another sword that had been dropped on the ground. It was just enough to throw me off balance. He caught me by the wrist as I fell and the larger man began to close in. "Two men", I thought.

Before the larger man could reach me, I shoved my knee into the groin of the man that had latched onto my wrist, stunning him just long enough for me to remove a dagger he had on his belt. I planted it deep in his chest and twisted it once for good measure. He let loose a strained groan and fell.

My father regained consciousness and immediately began pleading, his voice murky and failing. "Run, boy! Run while you still can! I'm already dead!" But the words rang hollow and impotent in my ears.

One man remained.

The last and largest of our attackers came forward. He considered the bodies of his four dead companions before giving me his full attention. "You've some fight in you, lad," he growled. "And you may think you know what you're doing with that sword. But, make no mistake - You will die on the end of my blade this day."

He came for me, drawing his dagger and throwing it at my throat. I easily sidestepped the dagger and reached out to pluck it from the air, only to realize my mistake at the last moment.

After throwing the dagger, he had launched himself through the air directly at me. Before I could react, he collided with me shoulder first, taking me off my feet, landing on top of me, and knocking the wind out of me.

I lay on the ground, crushed beneath him, gasping like a fish. He then reached back with one of his great fists and smashed my face. There was a bright flash of light and an enormous amount of blood. He'd broken my nose. By sheer force of will, I remained conscious.

He stood and picked me up by my wrist. My father's voice had become muddy and desperate. He pleaded hoarsely, begging the man to release me.

"Shall I kill him first, old man? Or should I let him watch his traitorous father die?"

"Please," my father whispered. "He's just a boy."

The man tightened his grip on my wrist, breaking it, causing me to yelp in pain. "Aye, he sounds enough like one. But no boy I've ever known could have done what he's done - four men laid low and not a scratch on him."

He walked forward until his and my father's noses were nearly touching. "It would be a mercy to grant him a quick death, no?"

"Please," my father whispered. "Just... just a child. Spare him."

The man lowered his voice, his teeth clenched. "The only thing I'll spare him is watching his cowardly father beg for his life."

He took two large steps back, held me aloft by my broken wrist, and drew back his sword to run me through. "You've shown yourself man enough to have earned some last words. Let's have..."

He stopped mid sentence and marveled as he watched the hairs on his arm begin to stand on end. The hair on his head also stood up all by itself. He looked about himself, distracted, momentarily unsure. My father cried out with his husk of a voice. "No, boy! You mustn't!"

The last man smirked and asked tauntingly "Mustn't what?"

I looked him in the eye and spoke a single word.

"Burn."

Lightning cracked from my hands and struck him in the face and shoulders. He dropped to the ground, smouldering, smoke pouring from his mouth, his eyes exploded from his head, the remainder boiling noisily in the charred hollows of his eye sockets.

The power soon overtook me using my anger as a conduit. I remained suspended in the air, crooked forks of lightning lashing out from all of me in all directions. It arched from every part of my being at once, annihilating the slain men on the ground, the grass, the trees, everything. The air was thick with hot sharp smoke, yellows and blacks and greys commingling, father and I obscured completely. My muscles contracted painfully, trying in vain to restrain the onslaught. The smell of burning flesh was everywhere.

Finally, I fell to my knees in the smoke and ruin about me. I had gone too far and was already preparing, yet again, to apologize to my father.

I called for him in the crackling and blinding chaos and heard nothing. Nearly all of the trees around us had caught fire. The smoke was as thick as wool. Disoriented and choking, I called to my father once more, straining against the pain of my broken wrist, searching through the suffocating smoke in vain. The last thing I heard before succumbing to the smoke was my father's voice, screaming in agony. I rushed toward him blindly, screaming, promising, begging, collapsing but knowing it was too late.

The fire had reached him.

The Call of His Name

I awoke face down, my hands balled into useless fists beside my head. Even before moving, I could feel how stiff and sore my body was. My cheek lay pressed against a cold hard surface, the taste of something like blood lingering in my mouth.

I thought, for an instant, that I had been in a fight and was coming back from a bad knocking down. But, with that, a stronger instinct announced that something different was wrong, though it could not name it. My mind seethed, casting attempts at recall into a void, retrieving nothing. I could not say what was amiss, but I became more sure of it the longer I lay still. Awake.

Eyes closed.

I felt the panic of uncertainty begin to seize me, and I focused on my breathing, slowing my heart rate, willing myself into calm. As the feral panic faded, my thoughts began to clear. I could hear the crackling of a nearby fire, the evening chirp and chittering of night things. I used it to ground myself and lay as still as I was able, stealing rhythmic shallow breaths. In time, it was enough to get my mind together, to focus.

I slowly opened my eyes to find myself in a large cage, raised a bit above the ground. I was stretched out on an iron floor heavy with the scent of some creature; likely the previous inhabitant of this cage. Flecks of paint or rust held like quivering leaves to the bars about me. Through the bars, I saw that the cage was resting on four sturdy wheels. I also saw a fire just a few feet away.

Looking much beyond the bars and into the world, adjusting my eyes, I began to see that early evening had just begun slinking into night. Great trees noisy with green, their arms spread wide, welcoming, trembling leaves made iron-black against the setting sun. I rubbed my eyes as they continued to slowly adjust to the light.

For an instant, I imagined a pair of overly round eyes evaluating me and my heart leapt, a panicked bird within my chest. This time, I allowed myself a brief moment of panic. Then, as before, I brought myself in submission to reason, resting within a ritual of breathing, listening, breathing.

I became aware of the smell of food and my stomach rumbled. I also was immediately aware that I was not alone.

It didn't talk long for me to gather that someone was holding me captive. And, in the next moment, it again became clear to me that there was very little that I *could* recall; shadows upon shadows, noises, smells - a disconnected tempest in an endless void.

I could not say where I was nor even speculate upon from where I had come - even my name lingered just out of reach, a rumor, a promise on the tip of my tongue. So much further was the idea of who might be holding me, much less why. Something like despair began to steal up on me. As I lay there struggling internally in the stillness, a ragged voice broke the silence:

> *I been down before*
> *Veteran of Love*
> *I have tallied the score*

The rueful tune was carried by a deep gravelly voice. As scared as I was, I yet noticed there were fragments of excellence and technique in his singing that suggested he must have at one time have been extraordinary, a marvel to listen to. Now, though, whatever sweetness had been was now thoroughly corrupted. The words came growling, a muddy haggard affair just short of animal sounds. It was the voice of a man long given to great shouts, old pipes, and cheap whiskey, a voice thick with scars and mucous and salt ridges, a worn and weary roar aggravated by bitter smoke and salty winds. It was the voice of a man well acquainted with strife and lies, keen to behoove or betray. It was, no doubt, the voice of the one that was holding me captive. And he had noticed me.

> *So I'll walk away*
> *And you'll close the door*
> *But any minute now*
> *You'll be wanting more*

After a moment, I noticed a shadow in the vague shape of a man lingering just beyond the fire. Though I couldn't discern its eyes, I could, nonetheless, feel its gaze upon me. We stared at one another over the fire in tacit palaver. Not taking my eyes off of the shadow, I slowly raised myself to a seated position. Taking my cue, the man-shadow rose and slowly began moving toward me, singing all the while.

Y'Make me call your name when you do that
Make you caaaaaaaaaall my name when I do this

As my eyes adjusted to the dim evening light, the shadow became a man. His face, partially hidden beneath the hood of his robes, was old and dark. Fixed deep within his dark constellation of skin was a pair of eyes, as cunning as they were clear. A splay of wrinkles retreated from the corners of his eyes like talons. Heavy creases ornamented the wide nose dominating the center of his face.

Won't you call my name when I do that?
Won't I caaaall your name... ever again?

He stopped singing, trailing off and narrowing his eyes as he closed the distance between us. Everything beneath his nose was hidden by a great dense beard of black and silver curls, braided here and there. At first glance, he appeared to be fat, very nearly waddling forward with an occasional inconspicuous wince of pain. But as he got closer, I saw the subtle promise of unrelenting muscle beneath the overindulgence. His arms were nearly as wide as his legs. I became aware of a dangerous sort of gravity about him.

Veins stood out on the back of his hands, straining against his skin, his fingers a tangle of knuckles that kept his hands as claws, fists, clubs. Distantly, I wondered how he'd set up camp, let alone how he'd managed to get me into this cage.

As he neared, I gathered myself to stand, and it was at that moment I became aware that my feet were bare. Indeed, an instant later, I realized that I was entirely naked. I felt another rush - this one of shame - and, on reflex, looked about me to see what I might cover myself with. Right away, I saw the animal skin upon which I had been lain. I snatched it up and covered myself.

When he reached my cage, he raised a hand to scratch absently at his beard and nodded his head toward the floor. I looked again and spied a clasp. While I struggled to secure the skin around me with this clasp, he spoke.

"My father taught me that song. Told me a colonist taught it to him." He smirked. "Couldn't have been true, but I believed it anyway."

Something in the way he spoke sounded familiar. I felt myself dropping my guard and pulled the skin more tightly about myself.

"That song - a stranger's song - was just about all that was left of him. Until now." This time, his subtle grin seemed to be hiding something sinister. I took a step back, my eyes fixed on him.

"Will you tell me your dream?"

After a moment or two seemingly lost in thought, he indicated with a knotted finger toward the rear of the cage, and the apparent source of the smell of food. A steaming bowl and hunk of bread sat on the iron floor.

"Eat", he said.

We stared at one another yet again, this time eye to eye. Half-starved, the food's scent was a powerful temptation. Nevertheless, I made no attempt to move. He stood there, considering me with dark impassable eyes. I became aware of my posture and immediately straightened up, easing my shoulders back and lifting my chin.

"Pride," he grunted, looking through me, then at me, gauging my understanding. Without warning, he reached between the bars and knocked over the bowl. Reflexively, I leapt toward the food and formed a dam around the steaming mess with my hands.

"Eat," he growled.

I abandoned what little dignity I had, bending over to devour the mess from the filthy floor of the animal cage. The bread was mealy and insect ridden, but I was undeterred, using it to wipe up what remained of the meal, bugs and all. In an instant, the whole mess had disappeared down my throat. I licked my hands clean, feeling stronger with food in my belly yet deeply ashamed.

The stranger motioned for me to return the bowl and I slid it across the floor of the cage. He reached between the bars and retrieved the bowl. He returned to the fire and refilled the bowl before returning to my cage. Then, he carefully maneuvered the bowl between the bars before placing it on the floor of the cage.

This time, I did not hesitate.

Not long afterward, it was full dusk. The sky - stained, bloody, oranges and purples mingled on the hem of the horizon, the sight filling me with a nameless longing. By then, the last smears of sunlight faded from simmering orange giving way to a deep indigo that seemed to push the stars back further than they should be. The fire cracked and sent up a shower of embers as the flames cast pantomimes of light and shadow against the trees on all sides of us. I could feel the stranger's eyes upon me as I slowly lowered the empty bowl from my face. He smiled and I was struck with an oddly familiar warmth, the vaguest echo of a memory. I didn't look away but I didn't return the smile.

"What's your name, boy?", he asked.

I opened my mouth to speak and nothing came out. Try as I might to recall, my name lingered just out of reach. A deep and foreign fear began to creep in. I hardened my face, steeling my gaze to hide my insecurity.

"Your name," he commanded again. "What do-,"

A wolf cried out in the distance, its long mournful howl ringing through the forest. The strange man's right hand flew to his scabbard, his eyes alert, his fingers fumbling. The wolf sounded off once more and the man returned to the fire, his hand now firmly grasping the scabbard of his sword. He cried out in a language I did not understand; it sounded like cussing. Then:

"Come, demon!" he shouted. "Come for me, you sonofabitch!"

The wolf's savage lonesome song rang out once again, louder, fuller, causing my heart to leap with fear and excitement - it was certainly getting closer.

Surrounded on all sides by bars, I moved toward the center of the cage. The stranger continued barking threats into the darkness, daring the wolf to attack, but his voice was nearly lost to me. I pivoted about, wary of the nearness of the bars, the black of night now seeming more present, not just dark now but also full of teeth. In the sky a thin silver disk of moon bathed the landscape in pale bone-colored light. I looked at the stranger again and was stunned.

He had cast his robes from his shoulders and stood bare chested, his robes held only by the tie about his waist. His scars had disappeared. The talons ornamenting his eyes had vanished along with every other telltale sign of aging. He stood taller, stronger, his chest and shoulders swelled outward, the whole of him renewed with young muscle. The sword hummed in the grasp of his sturdy and flexible fingers as his eyes glowed with a deep and secret light.

I could not look away.

The wolf cried out, much closer this time, a dark and lush refrain. The song went on, up and out in all directions, puckering my skin with cold fear. The song went on, endlessly rich for an eternity.

Then there was quiet. Infinite quiet.

We waited in thickest silence, he with a fist wrapped white-knuckled around the hilt of his sword, I shivering behind bars, both of us sweeping the forest with our eyes. The air was unnaturally still, the quiet dark somehow denser, closer, conjured all manner of illusions. We both stood watch in silence - he a titan out in the open, and me, a caged animal, the both of us quivering sentries smothered in the velvet dark of the evening forest, scanning the nothingness with shining anxious eyes. When at last satisfied that the wolf had gone, he relaxed, purging any remaining fear with a long slow trembling breath and letting his hand fall from his sword. In an instant, he was as he had been; aged, stiff, battered.

Sneering, he returned his gaze to me. I backed away to the opposite end of the cage until my back strained against the cool metal bars, the wolf forgotten entirely. He snorted and considered me openly, cocking his head slightly to one side, frowning with the effort of his concentration.

"You don't know, do you?" He continued to search me. "No. I suppose you do not." He casually grabbed the bars of the cage and continued. "I am called Arthur."

The light of the fire shone in the eyes of a wolf, not 40 yards behind him, staring at me with regal golden eyes. For a moment, I imagined the wolf leaping over the fire and tearing him apart. But it was a fleeting notion, nothing more. I wished him no harm. I only wanted to be out of the cage. And what, I thought to myself, should happen to me if he died? Where would I go? I did not know. I could not know. I stood perplexed.

The stranger called Arthur grunted, relaxed his grip on the bars, and brushed his hands against the front of his shirt. He considered me for a moment longer before turning his attention toward the fire.

"He's close," Arthur droned in a whisper. "But he's as scared as you are."

A memory rushed suddenly into the void. I heard a voice, patient and kind but growing weary nonetheless:

-can see myself, becoming... whole again...

"Huh?" I closed my eyes to capture it but it had already evaded me.

Seeing my confusion, he furrowed his brow. Then, "We'll talk more in the morning."

The memory vanished like smoke - the harder I tried to grasp it, the more ephemeral it became until there was nothing, until I'd lost even the meaning of my searching. I remembered the wolf and scanned the place I'd last seen him. Seeing nothing there, I turned and looked all around, hoping for some sign of the animal. I saw nothing.

The stranger called Arthur grunted. "You're wasting your time," he said, adding wood to the fire. "He's afraid of the fire."

Despite the haughty assuredness in his voice, he nevertheless took a long cautious look about himself before tossing more wood on the fire. The flames cracked and rose higher, brighter. Pleased with the fire, he spat on the ground.

"Rest," he commanded, yet the authority seemed diminished from his voice. He cleared his throat, momentarily unsure, before adding "We leave at first light."

I gathered myself into a ball in the center of the cage, trembling with questions. This time, I saw the wolf beside a tree, resting on its haunches, watching us. "Please don't kill him," I thought. "Not until he's let me out of this cage. The beast yawned with its enormous mouth before turning to disappear into the black of the woods.

Interlude: Watchman

Shadrach was hungry, and the smell of the stew was compelling. It wafted across the field of tall grasses penetrating the woods and finding him, even in his secret place. He tried at first to ignore it, to focus his thoughts on watchfulness, mindfulness. Yet that smell persisted, a continual beguiling imperative appealing to his baser instincts.

He paced a bit before dropping to his haunches to lay down, tucking his snout beneath his hind parts. He told himself that the food was spoiled, poisoned by the touch of the old man. He did all he could to steer his thoughts away from the scent, but found himself assaulted by it, even with his nose obscured by his hindquarters. After a time, he relented somewhat and stuck his nose into the air to better savor the portentous aroma. He snorted, drawing in several short whiffs of the fragrance and whined, immediately regretting the change in himself. Sampling the tainted air had only made his hunger more prominent, more needful than before. He stood and began pacing again, tortured by the stink from the old man's pot on the fire.

The hunger was as yet within his ability to manage, but he knew that it would not remain this way. Hunger only ever grew, creating ever expanding emptiness that wanted only to be filled and satisfied. Worse, the subtle creeping hunger that lingered just beneath his conscious thoughts, would occasionally emerge and cause him to transgress his better senses. Given enough time, it brought about in him tendencies of anxiety and impatience.

Yet so gradual was the erosion of his patience and composure that, often, he would err before coming into full awareness of his diminished faculties. Usually the fault cost him little, most often a meal. In the throes of intense hunger, he had a habit of making himself known to prey too soon, needlessly forcing a long chase that could have easily been a quick kill. Each time, he would feel the familiar pang of regret, panting and lunging in full stride, calling upon and wasting strength he did not have yet desperately needed, knowing full well he had only himself to blame for the gratuitous exertion. And, while the hunger that spoiled his self-possession also inspired a tenacity in him that was otherwise beyond his reach, the kill and meal that followed felt somehow exorbitant and wasteful, something gained in spite of his fault rather than because of his competence.

He thought back to a young deer he happened upon near the early part of his journey, how he had taken her cleanly and quickly in his jaws, granted her a quick death, and fed to complete fullness. He remembered leaving her carcass behind, how she had looked, slivers of moonlight suspended in the depths of her dark shimmering eyes, her bones snatched clean of flesh, rose-red stains of blood blackening her hide and the earth about her. He thought of the soft glistening viscera he had left behind, the skins and veins and fatty bits clinging to the white of her frame. He thought of all the things he could have and did not eat, now rotting in a field made improbable with distance, now eaten by some other creature or turned to dust. He could have, and did not, and now regret lay heavy like shame upon him.

The smell seemed to grow stronger and Shadrach felt his resistance wane. It reminded him of the smells that accompanied the seasonal festivals long ago held in Ashmane. While he had generally made a habit of avoiding the obnoxious affairs, he had, on occasion, been driven by curiosity to poke about the perimeter of the grounds in the night. The field would be crowded with tents of all sizes, lit from within by oil lanterns, men and women made shadows cast dancing against the illuminated sides. He'd observe tendrils of smoke rising like spectral fingers from piles of abandoned embers while fires great and small raged in their capacity, corralled by earth and stone. There were slabs of meats of varying sorts, each skewered on a length of iron and turning slowly, sporadically issuing drops of fat to hiss and sizzle on the embers below.

And there was music - all the day and night music - a tangled cacophony of instruments and clapping, chaotic choruses shouting, sustaining an endless spree of joy and revelry. Of all the noise and bother the festivals would bring, it was those slabs of meat that Shadrach now recalled most clearly. He yawned and let out another whimper of frustration as he looked toward the old man's fire.

He knew that he could easily sneak into their camp, steal food, and be gone before there was a response - his young muscles assured him of this. Yet, many days from anything resembling a meal, his body might be relying on the memory rather than the truth of that strength. Raiding the camp, even secretly, would no doubt further aggravate the already agitated and anxious old man and would almost certainly put the boy's life at risk. So, strong or not, he would have to keep his distance. Still, he was hungry. Very hungry. He whined, licking his chops.

Fixing his eyes on the old man in particular, Shadrach felt himself stiffen with anger. As he had several times before, he fantasized about killing him, shredding the old man's forearms with his fangs, snatching his knotted hands from his wrists, parting his midsection, watching as a rush of pink-grey guts tumbled out to lay steaming in the dirt. Shadrach imagined, at long last, tearing his throat out, feeling the spray of blood on his muzzle, the wet crunch of windpipe in his powerful jaws the old man flailing like an injured bird, uselessly beating his arms against Shadrach's sides, his panicked eyes jammed open in horrified desperation. He growled and began pacing a little. "Soon," he thought to himself.

Shadrach's stomach rumbled and he whimpered, licking his chops once more. He did not want to take his eyes off of the boy but he had no choice. It had been two days since he'd last eaten. He continued pacing, staring intently at the pair and willing the old man to sleep. After an eternity, the old man began to prepare for bed. Shadrach watched as he propped himself against a tree, stretched out his legs, folded his arms, tucked his chin into his chest, and closed his eyes. Within minutes, he was snoring gently.

Shadrach again began fantasizing about raiding the camp for food and, once again, decided against it. The frayed edges of sunlight blurred into evening across the horizon as he gave the old man one last look. Satisfied that the old man was asleep, Shadrach perked his ears up and stuck his nose to the ground.. He hoped for a few rabbits but knew he was not likely to be so lucky. Chances are, tonight, he would be dining on mice. Again. He told himself it did not matter, only the boy mattered. Still, the thought of chasing mice all night made him weary in advance. He whimpered yet again before drawing a deep breath and setting off into the night, hoping for rabbits.

#

Morning came early. Shadrach watched as the boy began to stir, ever so slightly, then, just as subtly, stopped. The young man was conscious but careful, feigning unawareness. To Shadrach, the change in his breathing was obvious. Still, he hoped the old man would not take notice.

Shadrach blinked slowly, his belly laden with mice and rabbits - 18 of the former and 4 of the latter. He had been exceedingly lucky and had overindulged, mostly out of anger. He had killed out of frustration and, having killed, ate, gorging himself, directing his rage at his meal. Now, as the sun crept over the horizon, instigating the nonsense chatter of birds and rustling of other day-creatures, all he could do was watch.

The old man began singing, an old song of death come too soon, of misfortune and regret, of youth met with unfortunate ends, of frailty and loss and the vanity of grief and self-pity. The large black mass of muscle and quills that had once been bound within the cage had finally returned to the shape of a small boy. No doubt, the boy would soon be awake. Shadrach watched as the old man slowly opened the cage and pulled the now loosed ropes from around the boy's naked body. He then carefully dressed him, taking great care not to jostle or otherwise disturb the child in a way that might awaken him. Afterward, he stood above the boy looking down on him, his head cocked to one side. To look at him now, it would seem as if the boy had only just fallen asleep there. The old man knelt down beside him and stroked his head once before kissing him on his forehead. He then stood and quietly exited the cage, taking great care to lock the cage behind him making as little noise as possible.

Shadrach's heart quickened. It would seem that the old man did remember. For a moment, he allowed himself to believe that, perhaps, his task wasn't as impossible as he had first believed. If the old man truly did remember, mayhaps the deed could be accomplished by simply asking him to let the boy go. Yet this fantasy was brief. Reality slowly crept in, reminding him of all he had seen. The old man had still locked the cage behind him. The boy was still his prisoner. And none of this would be undone by anything so simple as a polite request.

Shadrach struggled to stay awake before laying his head on his forepaws. "Mayhaps it is that simple," he thought. "Gods let it be so." He closed his eyes and let out an exhausted sigh. "Gods let it be so," he thought and allowed himself to be carried off to sleep.

Strike: A Dream

"Strike." he commanded. "Again."

My father stood in front of me without armor, his hands in his pockets. As I had been taught, I concentrated on my balance, his height, the distance between us, the weight of the sword in my hands. His eyes were sharp and focused, cold. He seemed to look at me and through me at once.

My first attempts had struck only air, vacant nothingness that once held my father's form. He read my intentions with ease, withdrawing from the edge of my blade like subtle smoke. Each failure invited his staff to strike my back, my shoulder, my hip, my crown. I was growing weary of it. My mind drifted for a moment and I imagined myself a great serpent, my mouth full of dripping swords, my father a quivering mouse. I wanted to hurt him, to earn

"Center yourself," he lectured. "Find the hollow space and fill it."

"Here at last I have found your hollow place," I thought. "I have summoned your emptiness and shall turn it against you."

With a convincing feint, I threw my weight forward as if to slash him, committing just enough to sell it as truth. For a moment, his eyes betrayed the slightest hint of fear, awareness, a glimmer of surprise. I shifted mid-stroke, turning on the ball of my left foot, drawing back with the momentum of the spin, and thrusting my sword at his belly. So confident was I that I regretted stabbing him in advance, preparing a haughty apology as recompense. Yet, at the last moment he sidestepped my blow and my sword passed harmlessly between his arm and his side. In an instant, I had been disarmed.

"You have the footwork of a seven year old boy," he said, handing me back my sword. "Do you suppose your enemy will take that into consideration? Perhaps he'll go easy on you? Maybe even offer you a starting blow?"

I was humiliated yet again, but knew that wasn't his intent. He was frustrated, yes, but there was a fear in his eyes that went beyond concern. I had to be better. Much better. I knew that, one day, we would have to face them. It was unavoidable. And I'd have to be better than the best of them if we were to survive.

He was preparing me. And I was failing him. I sighed heavily, sheathing my sword and nodding.

"Save your breath."

I started to reply but thought better of it and nodded instead.

"Strike," he commanded. "Again."

I drew my sword and centered myself.

Find the hollow space and fill it.

I drew a breath and struck again.

#

Our first fight happened in Dav Staggom and quite by accident. One of the old blacksmith's sons, Dane, felt I had insulted him and challenged me to a duel. I thought father would step in to defend me. Instead, he held out his hand. "You'll not fight as well with that cloak on, boy," he said. I handed him my cloak and heard him speak two words just above a whisper.

"Show him."

It wasn't long until a crowd had gathered. People began placing bets and exchanging money. I saw my father put the last of our few coins on the line.

Dane was drunk and I made short work of him. Twice, I was able to strike him on the collar bone with the flat of my blade. Once on the top of the head. Once on his rear end. Finally, I struck him flat on the wrist, breaking it and disarming him. The crowd that gathered cheered and began mocking him. Enraged, the man charged me, roaring like a lion. I tripped and tackled him, pinning him to the ground by his shirt sleeves with my daggers in one smooth motion.

The crowd cheered madly but our celebration was short lived. Father noted that the guards were likely to be summoned and the last thing we wanted was their attention. So we quickly gathered our winnings, purchased provisions, and fled.

It was a long while before we entered another city, again out of necessity, and I fought then as well. Soon after that, I fought again in Chevvar, and Elspud, and Dutney. The stage was set for a proper battle in Altrion but the fight was delayed due to a lightning storm. The next day, the crowd was three times the size but had attracted the attention of the guards. Desperate though we were, we simply could not risk it. Crestfallen, we vanished like mist after daylight.

We had much better luck in Wheelock. A festival was being held and with it, a tournament. The legitimacy of the event gave us confidence; there'd be no need to skirt the guards this time.

"The tournament is for Knights only," dad said. "But events like these bring the riff raff out. We should have no problem finding a challenger."

By mid-afternoon, we had already had three. A sizable crowd had formed and, as usual, we took that as a sign that it was time to leave. From the thick of the crowd came Dane, favoring his wrist where I had struck him with the flat of my blade months ago.

"Leaving so soon?" he asked.

"I'm afraid so," Dad said, still packing, paying the man little attention. Dane's hand shot out to grab my father's wrist. With his left hand, Dad batted Dane's hand away. At the same time, Dad grabbed on to Dane's injured wrist with his right hand and squeezed. Dane squealed with equal parts pain and surprise.

"Is there something else you wanted?" Dad asked, unruffled, calm.

Dane tried to retain an air of toughness and confidence. "I know you remember my face, fighter. You and that boy of yours fled like the devil himself was at your heels the minute the guards came poking about… just after you'd *stolen* my money."

"Lacking a man's courage does not mean that you cannot at least wear your defeat like one," dad growled. "You were beaten in a fair fight."

Dane's eyes were panicked but determined. "According to whom? A drunk and his whelp?"

Dad tightened his grip and Dane dropped to his knees, cursing. "I'm listening," Dad said.

"I want a chance to win my money back. One fight - a fair one this time... your boy and a man of my choosing."

I could almost see the wheels in dad's head turning, planning multiple escape routes, debating whether or not he could get away with killing Dane. Dad's eyes had gone cold. Dane didn't know it but he had forfeited his life the moment he threatened us. Dad lifted Dane to his feet, still holding him by his injured wrist, and pulled him in close enough to speak into his ear.

"You were beaten fairly ," he said. "Leave us be."

"Around here, a man gets a chance to earn his money back," Dane replied through a strained grimace. "Perhaps fair play isn't a concept where you come from?"

Even though his mind was still whirring, searching for alternate outcomes, I could see that Dad was beginning to realize that we'd either have to fight this man's challenger or try to flee. There was no doubt that we would have better odds with fighting. Nevertheless, his practical blood screamed that it was time to leave. We had more than we needed.

I watched as dad gave Dane another look, realizing that, even as soft as Dane was, his subtle threat left us in no position to argue.

"," dad said. "You have earned your one fight." He squeezed Dane's wrist more tightly. "One *fair* fight. Are we understood?"

Dane nodded his head vigorously like a child.

"One fight and we leave town for good with no need to look o'er our shoulders."

"None at all. You have my word."

"That I do," Dad said. "See that you keep it."

My challenger was much bigger than the others had been. Sizing him up, I made a quick note of his weaknesses. He was favoring his left leg a bit, his knee slightly red and swollen. By his squinting, I guessed he was nearsighted. He was holding an axe with both hands when he was clearly strong enough to heft it with one. One of his hands was sore, likely from pounding his axe against the shield of his last opponent.

On the other hand, he was built like a bear. That axe had no doubt drawn plenty of blood before. This man was a brawler, which meant he'd come after me relentlessly and do his best to keep me close. He'd eventually overwhelm me if I didn't end the fight quickly.

Father stood on the edge of the circle wearing a look of cool confidence. I briefly met his gaze and he stared at me as if he were already celebrating a victory. I braced myself and nodded at my opponent.

He came after me, lumbering forward wordlessly. Almost immediately, he made for my head with the axe. I ducked out of the way only to feel his fist on the side of my face. He was much faster than I'd guessed. I reeled only for a moment before regaining myself. He smiled a crooked broken smile and swung the axe again.I ducked again, hoping he'd try for a sucker punch.

He did.

I caught him by the wrist, stepped toward him, and flipped him over my hip.

Still holding his wrist, I stomped his face twice before he could regain himself and put some distance between us. If he felt any pain, I could not know. His face betrayed nothing save that crooked smile.

He was up in a flash and quickly closed the distance between us. I braced myself, preparing to dodge an axe swing but he kept coming, crashing into me and sending me flying. I hit the ground like a stone and the wind left me. Even before I looked I knew he'd be coming to pummel me. I rolled to the right on instinct and heard the blade of his axe bury itself into the earth just beside me. I estimated he was four steps away.

I lept to my feet and felt a strong urge to find my father in the crowd, to be granted permission to do what I intuited must be done. I was not sure. And I was beginning to lose my nerve.

"Find the hollow place and fill it."

"Death is inevitable. Victory is earned."

Noticing my momentary distraction, my opponent thundered toward me, swatting me into the air, and retrieving his axe from the earth with a grunt.

I didn't feel the rainfall until I hit the ground.

I looked into the crowd for my father and could not see him. I heard the brute stomping toward me, raising his axe for a fatal blow.

That I resisted with all my might does not matter. That, even unseen, I yet heard father's voice cry out, "No, boy! You mustn't!"

"You don't understand," I thought to myself. "I cannot. It is…"

The axe came parting the air, singing, mineral still and cool, already stained with raindrops.

"…a storm."

I held up an arm in self defense. Lighting fell upon him in a column.

The impact was enough to arrest his muscles and burn him to nothing in his armor. The lightning that had speared through him remained, undulating, twisting, arcing out to crasses my face, my arms. I stood, my arm still raised.

First, there were screams. Then, a stampede.

People fled in all directions, trampling one another, some even turning back long enough to hook a finger at me and yell "Rebuked!" before vanishing into the throng.

I felt dad before I heard him.

Be still.

Breathe.

Know that you are not alone.

I am with you.

Breathe as I do.

The column evaporated, leaving a heavy smell of char, ozone, and adrenaline.

I fell backward and father caught me.

"Run," he barked.

I did not need further encouragement.

Taken

I was jostled rudely from my dream, unexpectedly tossed and tumbling through the air before slamming hard into the unforgiving iron floor. For a moment, I felt pulled toward something, the pain still radiating from where my buttocks made violent contact with the hard floor. But, as the pain faded, so did the mysterious pull, as did the interest to explore it. Shaking it off after only an instant, I struggled instead to focus my eyes and determine where I was.

I could only manage to see enough that the cage and I were in motion. As I attempted to sit up, the ground bucked twice beneath me, knocking me off balance each time. I waited a moment, adjusting to the rough ride before trying again to right myself and have a look around. I became aware of the grinding of wheels against a dirt road as I rubbed my eyes, willing my vision into focus.

I was surrounded by thick iron bars on all sides. Above me was a weather wooden roof, beneath me the soft bristles of animal fur. The cage jumped twice more, throwing me once again. I recovered quickly and rebalanced myself on my forearms and knees, turning to face the direction in which the cart was being pulled.

In front of me was another wall of bars covered on the outside by planks of old wood, weathered, warped, and lousy with knots and splinters like thorns. High up on this wall was a small square window carved through the planks and covered on the other side with what I gathered must be a sliding panel. I approached the bars to the right of me and tried in vain to pass between them. Then, holding the bars, pulled at them, hoping against hope that they might give, but they would not yield. I held onto the bars, searching my head for another solution.

Without warning, the cage jumped yet again, yet, as I was still holding on to the bars, I was not thrown. Once and then again the wheels struck something, although this time, the knocks were accompanied by new sounds - the first a strained creaking groan, the second a clang of metal against metal - and then naught but stillness overlaid with the steady din of wheels over earth. Again, I settled before continuing.

I looked once again to the rear of the cage and noticed a gap between the two bars that met to form the rear right corner. And, while it was by no means large enough to squeeze through, it revealed where the door of the cage could be found. As I looked closer, I saw that the entire rear portion of the cage served as the door, hinged at the top, middle, and bottom on one end and fastened shut with two large locks at the other. Whatever had last jostled the cage had also forced the lock at the top right of the cage to give way. Now, each time the cage was upset with adequate force, the rear gate clanged noisily. Knowing that it was only a matter of time before the old man steering us also became aware of the sound, I rushed over on all four to examine the lower lock.

It was apparent at once that the top lock, thoroughly rusted with age, had broken, shaken apart by repeated jarring. The bottom lock looked no sturdier than the other, and I grinned - escape, it would seem, was possible. I had only to wait until the front wheels of the cage hit another obstacle, and then properly time the rear wheel striking the same with a kick to the lock. I looked about for animal skin, tucked it beneath my arm, and waited for the next collision.

The first came quickly and, though slightly out of sync, I kicked the lock when the rear wheels struck an errant stone. A shower of red dust fell from the lock but it held fast. I drew a breath and, when the time was right, kicked again, this time much harder than the last. Yet, for the full force of my effort, I was rewarded only a second and smaller drizzle of dust. In all, I was able to kick the lock five times. Each time thrusting my heel at the lock with all my might, each time producing progressively smaller sprinklings of reddish dust and nothing more.

Panic came then, threatening to take hold for good. Desperate, I stood, wrapped myself in the animal skin, backed myself against the front of the cage, and then charged the rear gate, throwing my full weight against it. This time, the lock gave a short high pitched groan, and a crack appeared in its casing. Without hesitation, I prepared to charge again.

Before I was able to gather myself, I was thrown headfirst against the front wall of the cage as it suddenly stopped short. I lay there, stunned yet nonetheless attempting to stand and charge once more. But the effort of standing proved too much and I fell to my knees on the floor of the cage, reeling. The top of my head throbbed. I touched a hand to it and it came back tacky with blood.

In spite of my being dazed, I hear the sound of horses - at least two - snorting and shaking their heads. As I crouched in the cage, stunned, I heard the sound of boots striking the ground. As I struggled to center myself, I began to think of how I might confront the old man, deciding I would demand his name and a reason why I was being held.

A surge of fear, indignation, and plain stubbornness granted me one last attempt at standing, but it was for naught. I rose on wobbly legs and managed to place my back against the wall, the jagged splinters biting like teeth into my flesh. I dug in my feet and prepared to charge,lunging forward with two confident steps before falling once again to the floor of the cage. I slunk back against the wall.

The steps slowed as they neared, finally stopping just beyond the right side of the cage. My fear was quickly joined with sadness and resignation - there'd be no escaping. I shook my head, still grasping at clarity, and slowly raised my eyes to meet my captor.

In his left hand, he held a length of rope, and in his right, a pair of sturdy manacles. After scanning the length of the cage, he fixed his full gaze on me, evaluating me with an impersonal gaze. I returned the gaze but made no attempt at a brave posture. I was, for now, defeated, and resigned myself to take a more subtle stance.

He walked to the rear of the cage, produced a key from his pocket, and unlocked the lower lock. The gate swung open with a pitiful groan and the old man examined the locks with a peculiar stare, one bushy eyebrow raised higher than the other. A growl rose in his throat, then he spat a wad of phlegm onto the forest floor and cursed. He looked the cage over yet again before sighing heavily and returning his gaze to me.

"Which will ye have? The cords?" he said holding up the rope. "Or the irons?" he said, raising the manacles.

I would have neither, but didn't dare to say so. "I'll have the cord."

He nodded knowingly, then swung the gate closed and, after a moment's hesitation, relocked the bottom lock. He motioned for me to walk toward him with my hands behind me. Then, he motioned for me to turn around.

"Sit," he barked. I placed my back to the bars on the side of the gate and slowly lowered myself to the ground. Then, I took my legs out from underneath myself and stretched them out in front of me.

He walked over to me and, reaching through the bars, roughly grabbed me by my wrists and yanked them toward himself. Pain shot through my shoulders but I remained silent. I heard him tying off one end of the rope but could not see. Thereafter, he bound my wrists together, then circled the rope around my left elbow, around my chest, and around my right elbow before tying off the other end. When he'd finished, he tugged one at the rope and I yelped in pain.

"I will return," he said and, after a pause, his footsteps began to disappear into the woods."

Without thinking, I struggled a bit against the ropes and earned myself more pain and another short howl of discomfort. "Wait!," I cried out. "Please! The wolf!"

Heedless of my cries, the sound of his footsteps diminished at the same rate, from crunching rhythm into nothingness.

Alone, I looked all around myself, first for fear of the wolf, then taken by the view of the forest itself. Behind and on either side of me beyond the bars was a suspended shower of bright green leaves, their edges shimmering with errant sunlight, dangling from a crowd of branches. The trees burst from the earth in smudged variations of reds and browns. Each stood on great tangles of roots, braiding and pushing at once into and from the black earth. Above was a web of golden light tumbling through the gaps in the forest canopy, falling to earth and rendered as a series of dusty golden pools choked with musty red-brown underbrush, the occasional finger of sapling green peeking through, young branches splayed, vibrant and tender-green. The path (such as it was) upon which we'd been traveling was a blackened artery stricken with errant roots and stones, pocked with gaping holes, astonished mouths haloed with clots of mud where the wheels had found them.

I tried again and again to remember my name, to take hold of anything familiar but could not. It wasn't long before I gave in to tears, great shaking sobs of helplessness and despair. It seemed that the memory of who I was and all I'd known lay just beyond my reach; I could feel it all there, just beyond me, obscured by an impenetrable fog - worse, reaching out only seemed to push things deeper. I was alone and a stranger to myself, weeping until I had no more strength to weep. Then, hanging my head, I resigned myself to sleep.

#

I awoke surrounded by the stink of rusting iron just as the afternoon began softening into early evening. My rest had calmed me and cleared my thoughts considerably. I felt much more aware of my surroundings, the smell of young grass and wet earth, a gentle wind heavy with the memory of rain, the faint echo of animal dung, the blood-rust stink of the iron. I was suddenly met with fresh pain and immediately began to struggle. The old man pulled down hard on the ropes. This time, I cried out.

"Be still," he growled, waiting for me to settle down before continuing to untie my bonds. Hearing him step away, I stood, slowly, rubbing at my shoulders and wrists all the while.

The stranger walked over to the remains of the fire, now a pile of glowing embers, and sat himself on a large stone. From where he sat, he pointed at the rear of the cage, jabbing the air with his index finger. I crawled toward the bowl and ate quickly. The food was warm. As subtle as I was able, I looked toward the lower lock at rear of the cage. The distance between the bars at the corner of the gate was just a bit wider than it had been before. He had opened the gate while I slept.

I wondered if he had remembered to lock it, and hoped the scheme didn't translate to my face.

He seemed to ignore me as I gobbled the meal, again finishing by licking my fingers and the bowl. Satisfied, I wiped my hands on the animal skin before wrapping it about myself. At this, he stood and approached the cage. I resisted the urge to retreat to the bars behind me and, instead, willed myself to stand my ground. Upon reaching the bars, he leaned in close, his eyes cloudy and unfocused.

"Tell me your dream."

I raised an eyebrow, confused.

"You struggled in your sleep, calling for your father." he said. "Tell me of it."

"I hardly slept at all," I said.

"No?"

I swallowed once. "I was afraid the wolf might return."

He grunted and handed me a water skin. I shuddered and began to drink.

The water tasted muddy but was nonetheless cool and refreshing. I drank deeply, doing my best to keep my eye on the stranger, stopping every now and then to catch my breath. For me, the night had been a blur of endlessly looping schemes and calculations. Between fitful periods of sleep, I tried desperately to weave together phantom threads of solutions but to no avail. My anxiety had almost nothing to do with the wolf and everything to do with escaping.

But he was right. In the moments that I slept, I did dream, though it lingered in my memory as a jumbled confusion of words and images. The fragile thoughts and impressions that remained haunted me completely yet disintegrated like scattered leaves when attended for more than a moment or tried to name them.

Worse, I had talked in my sleep. I thought then that he must know what I had dreamed, and was only mocking me. I felt vulnerable, ashamed, imagining what else I might have revealed in the night. With all that was on my mind, I was sure I must have given him enough to counter any plan I might come up with.

"We cannot control how the past returns to us."

A thought, a feeling, passed through me and was quickly lost. The wind shifted and the strange metallic scent filled my nostrils once more. This time, I recognized it as blood. "The wolf," I said. "The wolf killed your mount."

"Mount? Heh." His jaw tightened and he spat on the ground. "*Your* wolf killed *my* horse," he said. "Scared the damned thing to death." He stretched, cleared his throat, and spat again.

I thought over the short summary of events that had led to this. And now... "My wolf?"

"Just as well," he said, ignoring me or not hearing me. "Would have died soon anyway, wolf or no." I immediately put the water skin back to my lips and watched as he waited, not without a little impatience.I paused again, gasping.

"The other is sick, as was the first," he began and then paused, searching for words. "...and so am I," he said finally. I again drank deeply from the skin.

"No doubt you have already figured that for yourself," he said.

It was my turn to ignore him. I continued drinking and furrowed my brow when the skin was finally empty, shaking it to be sure. Satisfied, I held onto the skin nonetheless. For a moment he stood there, his hands bunch into fists.

"Quite finished?" he asked.

I drew a breath to respond just as he vomited forcefully and suddenly.

Dredge

I looked away almost immediately, yet could still hear the sound of his retching. The noise came again, a desperate garbled animal sound, followed by splatter, panting, gagging, cursing.

After it seemed that it was over, I looked again and saw him bent over, his hands on his knees, panting, a thin strand of drool hanging from his mouth. A few moments passed like this before he slowly began to stand to full height, cursing and wiping his mouth with his sleeve. Before he could fully right himself, he suddenly vomited again, spraying blood and half-digested food onto the ground. This time, he stared at the mess, swaying on his feet, his mouth agape, vomit lingering in his beard. His breath came in great, slow, deliberate gasps. Great blooms of panicked blush spread across his face. He stood like that for a while, catching his breath, readying himself for another attack.

Without warning, he vomited once more and doubled over, clutching his belly, groaning in agony. His eyes began to glaze over and he fell over hard on his side, breathing like a wounded animal. Before long, he was racked by another stomach crap, this one much more painful. His angry measured growl lost its controlled edge and took on a more helpless plaintive tone.

"A howl," I thought but did not say.

He eventually fell to his knees. Then his side. Then he was silent, apart from occasionally quivering and lowing sickly. He slowly away from the bloody mess before settling on his side, heaving slowly, near stillness interrupted only by the occasional punctuation of a pained groan.

I realized in that moment just how trapped I was. One of the horses that pulled the cage was dead and the other was soon to follow. Likewise, the old man that held me captive me was dying. Should he not survive, I'd be left to starve to death alone in a cage in these woods. Should he survive, I'd be left to his devices.

My choices, few as they were, became clear to me.

Though lost and ignorant, I could attempt an escape and hope to find help. I knew enough to follow running water (though did not know *how* I knew) and I'd eventually find people. But there was no telling what sort of people I would find. And if I were to injure myself while running mostly naked in the woods, if I were to break a leg or become poisoned, I would risk dying alone. Yet it seemed to be the most reasonable course of action. No man who would keep another in bondage could mean him well. Wherever we were going, it was, at least, against my will and, likely, against my best interests. But I was alive. And, as yet, being kept alive.

The thought of not escaping would have seemed to me a day ago to be utter nonsense. But now, considering all things, it was almost comforting. He had fed me and didn't seem to have any intention of killing me. He must need me alive and relatively unharmed, else he wouldn't have bothered to see to it that I was fed.

As he wrestled with whatever sickness had taken him, I could only feel frustration and sadness at my inability to help myself. He whimpered once more, the self-conscious pretension entirely eroded from his pain, and I was again consumed by a rush of emotion. I loosened my grip on the bars and sat down.

After a few minutes of silence, he straightened up, combing a hand through his beard and wiping it on his shirt. Then, growling, he half-heartedly kicked some dirt over the mess he made. Ambling toward the remains of the fire, he suddenly seemed much older. He knelt by some saddlebags and rummaged for a bit, eventually pulling out a reddish brown root.

Seeming sure that the worst of it had passed, he took the root, bit off a large piece of it, and chewed vigorously. For a while he sat quietly, resting on his knees, his head bowed. Before long, he stirred a little and stood up. The sharp rank stench of vomit hung in the air all around us. Once again, he raised the red-brown root to his mouth and began chewing it. Gradually, the color returned to his cheeks and his breathing eased.

"You're dying," I said.

He smiled a pathetic, old man's smile. "Don't get your hopes up, lad." He spat on the ground once more. "If there are any Gods still ruling this world, I suspect they're keeping watch over both of us." He looked at me, through me for a moment, as if I were a ghost. "Surely, they wanted me to find you."

I cringed unconsciously, unsure of what he meant.

He growled up a large wad of phlegm and spat upon the ground, staring at the mess he'd made before continuing. "Before I've surrendered to the crows, I mean to finish what I started. And I intend for you to help me."

"Help you? "

"By rights, I should have split you open and left you right where I found you. You'd earned as much. But I'm giving you a chance - the Gods have given us both a chance to mend this."

I spoke quietly. "Mend what?"

"The world," he said, his voice trailing off a bit, distracted. "A chance to mend the world…"

"What if I--"

"I'll gut you," he said flatly. And I'll toss you in my pot."

He let the threat linger in the air a moment before pulling out a tobacco pouch and busying himself with stuffing a long pipe. "Or," he began again, "I'll leave you here. To sort out those locks and bars."

He paused again to examine the pipe. Satisfied with his work, he lit it and drew deeply, exhaling as he spoke. "Though I reckon you wouldn't still be on that side of the bars if you were the tinkering type."

My back stiffened. "You still need me. Otherwise you would have left me to die. Or killed me. Certainly you'd not have shared your meal so easily."

He grunted. "Oh?"

"A man desperate as you are is in no position to bargain for the truth. And you're at least desperate enough to call upon a caged boy for help. But this nonsense of vague mysteries serves neither of us. I cannot help without knowing. Therefore, you are either a liar, and will show himself as such, or you are not, and will see reason to speak plainly."

"Or I am shrewd," said, "and you misjudge me."

He wiped his mouth and set his eyes on me.

"Don't fret. You'll have an answer, boy." he said. "By word or by deed. Not that it matters. Though you might believe that you are without a reason to trust me, your circumstances dictate that you must." He gestured toward the empty bowl that had held my soup, and the water skin from which I drank. "Your actions tell as much." I looked at them again for the first time, somewhat unsure.

"You're a smart boy, but not enough to know when you've been bested." Before I could compose a response, he shifted a bit and leaned to one side, his face contorted. For a moment, it seemed he would be sick again. Instead, he let out a long low burp. He trailed off, lost, distracted by errant thoughts.

"What now then?" I said.

"Now?" He tapped the stem of the pipe against his teeth a few times. "Well *now*, it would seem, I hold all the cards. And *now*, I would very much like to have your name, pup."

I thought quickly. "I am called... I am..."

He raised an eyebrow. I stared into his eyes, boldly returning his challenging gaze. He smirked and began laughing.

"No name? No dreams? Are you sure you're a man at all?"

I bristled but remained silent.

He grinned and narrowed his eyes slightly. "I suspect you're beginning to appreciate the position you're in. Do as I ask, and live." He stood and began walking over to my cage. "Or, you might try my patience."

He placed his hand on the pommel of his sword. "In which case, if I am in a generous mood, I'll aid you in crossing over swiftly. Though, as it stands now, I'm inclined to avoid the mess and leave you there to count your ribs."

He drew in a lungful of smoke and exhaled from his nostrils. "How's that for 'what now'?"

I swallowed once and remained silent.

After what seemed like an eternity, he spoke again. "There is a creature East of here hiding in a small village "Halverson's Notch"; the creature has many names but it is called "Ogmwa" by those who are fond of it. He narrowed his eyes, spat on the ground, and continued.

"As I've said, you are all that remains of my father. Should I survive our journey, I mean to see the creature killed. I mean to see his heart torn from his chest and set afire."

"And you need my help," I said.

"Make no mistake, boy, that demon will meet its end with or without your help. So, yes, I'll have your help. Or your life. Fine to settle for either."

This time, the threat didn't seem as sincere. The thought of my helping him had begun to obscure his passion for ending my life. I decided to nurture the former. "What must I do?"

He smiled wickedly. "There's a boy." He drew another lung full of smoke and continued. "I have been dispatched to destroy this monster and have every intention of doing so. However, I've since heard tell that the village has grown rather protective of its monster, so much so that they now go to great lengths to protect it. Moreover, due to… other complications… they are expecting me."

"Rather," he continued, "what they're anticipating is a man traveling alone, a sturdy warrior well suited to rid the world of the evil such as that which dwells in their village. They'll likely take no notice of a dying old man and a young boy."

He drew from the pipe again, and stared at me in quiet contemplation. Then, blowing smoke from his nostrils, he raised an eyebrow. "Indeed. If we're careful with our charade, they might even welcome us."

I lowered my eyes, considering all he had said.

He stood and bit down on the pipe. It looked as though it were suspended in his beard. "In exchange, not only will I spare your life, I'll keep it."

I looked at him, conflicted. All roads from here seem destined to intersect with death.

"As your keeper, I swear no harm shall come to you - none that won't have to pass through me first" He looked me in the eye and touched his heart with his right hand and then touched his lips. Before I knew what I had done, I touched my right ear with my right hand and then touched my heart.

"Aye", he said. "So it's not all gone." He smiled broadly. "That was a promise made. Good to see your mind is returning. No doubt more will come to you in time."

After a moment or two, he strode toward the rear of the cart and began to unlock the gate. Then, pausing, he looked up from the lock. "And have I your word, boy?"

My head spun with questions. There seemed to be no good choice to make. But I could not remain here. "No manacles," I said finally. "No manacles nor bonds of any kind.

He nodded. "Very well."

"And I'm to be freed once the deed is done. Unharmed." I paused before adding "And-"

"Don't go mistaking this for a negotiation, boy," he interrupted. "We are by no means on even terms."

The thought of starving to death alone, trapped in a cage was a compelling one. Yet even that was not enough to keep me from pressing once more. "And... and you will tell me all you know of who I am, where I am from, and anything else that might... that could..."

My eyes stung with tears, and I felt another wave of sorrow wash over me. I wept silently, ashamed of my tears yet unable to hold them back. He looked away from me, for a brief moment sharing in my shame, before drawing on his pipe again and spewing smoke. He made a face as though he might fire an insult or dismissal, but it did not hold. Instead, he softened slightly, running his right hand through his beard and staring at me with something like sincerity.

Then, "Understand, I do not undertake this journey lightly. And it is a hell of a thing to wake in the middle of a war, unarmed. But here you are. And here we are. Understand?"

He must have seen me calculating and leaned forward in response.

"If I stood any chance of facing this devil alone, I wouldn't have... you would have been left alone. I cannot apologize for a deed I have no intention of making right. This is a wrong thing that I do, but for the right reasons. And I cannot explain it all - there's not enough of you there yet. Know now that you'll be released once the deed is done. And you will part from me knowing all that I know of who you are. And you'll be under my protection." He paused briefly before adding, "You have my word."

I sighed heavily and returned his nod. "You have my word also."

He stepped to the rear of the cage and pulled at the gate, swinging it open. I hesitated for a moment. He had not unlocked the gate but simply pulled it open. My initial suspicion was confirmed. It had been unlocked. I considered what might have happened if I had said no, and could not imagine that he would have relocked the gate. I reasoned that, had his threat been sincere, he would not have unlocked the gate until he had secured my word in advance. His threat of leaving me to starve alone in the cage had been little more than a bluff, and a poor one at that. More than that, it seemed that he had intended to let me go whether I eventually agreed to help him or not. But why? Why would he-

"Let's be off then, son," he said, interrupting my thoughts. "There's a wolf about."

As I stepped toward the rear of the cage, I tried to return to my thoughts but could only focus on the open gate before me. "Why," I thought, before the notion was overshadowed by the sudden fear that my hesitations might cause him to change his mind. Spurred by this, I bounded the last two steps toward the gate. Then, pulling the animal skin tightly about myself, I drew a deep breath and leapt out of the cage.

Interlude: The Wild

Shadrach continued to observe from a distance. He had become somewhat confident that the boy wasn't in mortal danger - not yet, anyway. Nevertheless he felt a quickening of his blood each time he cast eyes upon the old man. His mind, governed by reason, usually kept his baser instincts in check, but his animal nature manifested bodily, causing his fur to bristle, his paws digging into the earth.

"Watch," he had been told. "See that no harm comes to him."

He had accepted the task with reluctance and only after repeated protests.

"I am young," he had complained. "I am as yet loyal to my instincts, rash, impulsive."

And there had been many that agreed with him: "There is too much of the wild left in him," they said.

But the task remained his. "Watch," he was told. "See that no harm comes to him." At that, he had bowed his head, still fearful and insecure but nevertheless conceding to the deed.

For days, there had been nothing. He had trotted through the forest somewhat aimlessly, filling his nose with empty air and whimpering like a lost pup. The scent he had been given had been especially distinct, and he had struck out from the pack confident that he would at least be successful in tracking it down. But, as the days and nights passed, he began to lose faith in his abilities.

Moreover, absence of the pack had lowered his morale considerably. More than once, he found himself conjuring excuses to return, just for a few days, perhaps to set out again, this time with Alistair and Wellfleet alongside him. Yet, as eager as he was to rejoin them, he was all the more determined not to disappoint them. So he pressed on in spite of his loneliness and doubt.

Happening upon them had been an accident. He had been asleep on his back, limbs akimbo, kicking at the air in the fit of some dream, when the noise of the empty cart roused him. He awakened with a start, turning himself over in a flash and pressing himself to the ground, his head swiveling this way and that. The old man and his cart had been the first humans he had seen since he set out, but that was not what caught his attention. It was the smell.

Having been startled, his senses had been on high alert, and, while he had expected the stink of the man, he had not expected to detect that distinct scent he had been given to find. In fact, it was, at first, so subtle as to almost be unfamiliar.

And yet, suddenly, there it had been! His eyes had lit up and he had nearly yelped aloud before catching himself. For a moment, he had forgotten his task and could only wriggle in excitement. And then, it had come to him again, slowly, as with the recollection of a dream.

"Watch. See that no harm comes to him."

Being fully occupied with attempting to pass off the task, he had asked no questions about the subject of his search. But now, looking upon the boy with his own eyes, he could not help but wonder who he might be. He became aware that his tail was wagging, and he stilled himself.

"Watch," he heard in his head. "See that no harm comes to him."

"Wait," he said to himself, and crept through the woods in a wide arc toward the old man's blind side, being careful to make as little noise as possible. Once well out of sight, he drew closer to them so as to discern their conversation.

Even from where he stood hidden in the thick of the forest, Shadrach could smell the horses the old man had burdened with hauling the cage. Yet their wild and natural animal smell was buried under a raw and sour stench of something sinister, a stink of sickness and impending death. Just beneath that awful smell was the sharp and unmistakable scent of fear. To Shadrach, it smelled of spent lightning and muddy stones. For a moment, he felt himself empathizing with the poor creatures, remembering his own fear.

The old man had no doubt picked up the animals back east - likely they had been young and strong, pulling the massive iron cage with ease, as if they were only marginally aware of the encumbrance. Yet, as they traveled with the old man, the animals began to show signs of ill health. Shadrach had approached the beasts in the night to speak with him while the old man slept. Though he knew the horses would smell him, he

...remained hidden in the tall grass, hoping not to panic the creatures.

"Hail, brothers."

The horses flipped their ears up in unison, the smaller one also snorting with surprise. "I am called Edward," the smaller horse offered. "I am no brother. You smell of danger, stranger."

"We are brothers, you and I," Shadrach said patiently. "I have come to help you, to free you from your master."

Edward looked around, anxious but not yet taken by fear. The larger horse drew himself up and snorted loudly, shaking his head. "It is a wild thing, Edward," the larger one warned. "It is a wild and dangerous thing that wants to kill us. It would eat us, it would."

Shadrach pressed further, "You are sick, brothers." He paused before adding, "The boy in your cage has caused it."

Edward brayed loudly, stupidly. "You are trying to trick me, Danger Stranger, but I am very smart. I and Oswald are very so much smart, aren't we, Oswald?"

The larger horse snorted and shook his head again, its tail swishing back and forth. "You are trying to fool us, but it is you that are foolish ever so much. You cannot to fooling us - you are no tame thing. Show yourself!" he squealed.

Shadrach crouched even lower, flattening his ears against his head. "Peace, brothers. The noise you're making is sure to wake your master. Surely he won't take such an offense lightly."

Oswald snorted once again, and was quiet. Edward paused also, lowering his ears and then his head. Then, quietly, "You are right, Danger Stranger. You are quite very much right."

Shadrach spoke even more softly, "As I've said, I am here only to help you, brothers."

For a moment, the horses seemed to understand. Shadrach continued. "I mean you no harm. Allow me to free you, brothers, to roam wherever you please, only far away from here. That man will be the death of you."

At this, Edward straightened up, seemingly struck by a brilliant idea. "Master will know! I shall ask him, Stranger Danger, and he will know because he is smart! He is so very much smart! You'll see!"

Shadrach began pleading again but it was much too late. Both Edward and Oswald began to whinny and strike out at the air with their hooves. Within moments, the old man began to stir slightly before quickly leaping to his feet, scabbard in hand.

"FOOLS!," Shadrach whispered, though he was sure the beasts could not hear. He slinked back into the forest, his retreat covered largely by the horses' commotion. The old man lit a torch from the embers of the fire and shone it about, searching the woods around them with great care. Edward had stopped then, a look of dumb animal pride on his face. After a while, satisfied that they were alone, the old man relit the fire and pulled his bed roll closer to its glow. But he did not sleep, instead, keeping watch all night, cautiously scanning the perimeter of the camp.

"You fools," Shadrach whispered again, this time to himself. "You simple fools."

In spite of the creatures' loyalty, Shadrach was still determined to help them. Yet, in spite of his passion to do so, he could not see a way of doing so that did not also put his own life at risk, not to mention the boy. As much as Shadrach did not want to allow it, he could see no other way.

He could not take the old man on. Shadrach rightly intuited that the old man was deadly with his bare hands alone. Moreover, Shadrach noticed the Tsenmaerd on the old man's waist, his hands never more than a slight lunge from the hilt - even the crudest and weakest became formidable foes when in possession of a named blade. In the old man's hands, Shadrach reasoned the old man could easily fend off a legion of men, let alone one young and angry wolf.

As the evening wind swept through the wood, bringing with it the scent of the old man's camp, Shadrach could smell the horses that were hauling the cage. The stink of death mingled with the raw sour stench of sickness was overwhelming.

It was only a matter of time, he reasoned. And time, it seemed, was on his side.

Shadrach smelled death on the old man but did not need the scent to know for certain. Each morning and night, the old man would wrestle with himself, racked by terrible pain, vomiting blood and bile, whimpering and groaning, savaged from the inside out. The mule flesh would only hasten this disease. In time, he would be too weak to stand up to the boy much less a young wolf. Shadrach could then easily take the boy without a fight.

"Watch," he heard in his head, and allowed himself to obey.

"Wait," he said to himself, and steadied his gaze upon them.

In the Dark

The first few days of our journey passed thus; by light we pushed through the wilderness, trudging over hills, ambling through pastures knotted with stone, stumbling over felled trees and hidden roots, the underbrush tugging at the hem of our cloaks. Sometimes, we'd travel a great distance only to circle back and continue in another direction. Other times, he'd carry me on his back. And, when we came upon a river, we'd wade into it and travel upstream or downstream (never directly to the opposite bank) before emerging cold and wet on the other side. Just before dusk, we'd make camp in a musty cave or a cluster of underbrush, or on the plain dry leaves beneath a stand of tall trees, or nestled into a dense clutch of bushes. Each time it was the same - no fire.

We brought the stew of mule flesh and tough vegetables with us, forcing the cold clotted mess down our throats until it ran out on the third night. After that, we ate when we could and whatever we happened upon; wild rabbits, berries, frogs. When we were lucky enough to come upon meat, he'd start a small fire and roast our kill, but only a dawn or dusk - never during the full light of day. More often than not, however, he'd dig a hole, start a small fire, and be sure it was out before the young down blossomed into full daylight.

Most times, after our meal, Arthur would disappear without explanation and remain absent for a time. Sometimes, he would only get a few steps away before vomiting. Other times, I'd listen from a distance as he emptied his guts with strained gurgling agony.

He did not always remember to bind me.

#

We had been headed in many different directions for many days, the landscape changing with limited variation. We were preparing to sleep when, as suddenly as usual, he was taken by the illness. In a moment, he had vanished, replaced by the heavy thud of retreating footsteps. Then, I thought I heard him fall to his knees, and the whole awful ceremony began again.

There was something alive in me, something more aware than I that begged me to run, to take advantage of his illness and be free. But there was something else as well, something hidden deep in the fog that I had yet to penetrate.

I decided to go to him.

He was much worse now.

I saw him on the ground, curled and shivering in the fetal position. He had lain in his filth, murmuring to himself. As I neared him, he made several feeble reaches for his sword, but it was pure instinct and no intention. He would always curl back, groaning, growling.

I reached toward him to put a hand on him; I didn't know what else to do. Before I could make contact, his head spun suddenly, fixing me with rheumy bloodshot eyes. He grunted something like 'Don't' before swatting my hand away.

He was greatly weakened but still strong enough to hurt me, even with a swipe at my hand. It was only an instant, that pain, but, for a moment, the fog suddenly lifted. I saw my entire self, how I came to be here, where we were headed, and why. Mostly, I saw him. I saw him clearly. And, though the fog returned as quickly and completely as it had been lifted, I managed to hold on to a few scraps of the vision;

We were not strangers. His name was not Arthur. And "Arthur" was operating beneath a fog of his own.

Even in his strained and bloodied eyes, I saw that he could tell that something had happened, something he had not intended. He growled and reached for his sword, this time with a surge of determination.

"Don't *ever* touch me."

I stepped backward, but did not flee. He reached for the sword again, but it had become an afterthought. I could see him beginning to fade, and felt a flicker of both excitement and fear; could I finally escape? And what would become of him?

After gurgling a few times, he stopped breathing and dropped face first into the filth. I didn't hesitate.

Grabbing him by his robes, I pushed and rolled him onto his back. I took care not to touch his skin, though the temptation was immense. The stench of the vomit, blood, and long-traveled old man were all making my gorge rise; I spat on the ground beside us and continued, reaching into his robes and producing the pouch that contained the root. When I went to put it into his mouth, I noticed he wasn't breathing - something was in his mouth.

Don't ever *touch me.*

I wrapped my right hand in part of his robes and, gritting my teeth, opened and cleared his mouth by hand; scooping gobs of gore of varying textures until there was nothing. I put my ear near his mouth, careful not to touch him, and thought that I heard shallow breathing. As I hovered, listening, he coughed himself loudly back to consciousness, both grabbing the hilt of his sword and striking me away with his new strength.

I was thrown against a tree and felt my left arm break. I lay there, watching him stand in the fullness of strength, barking threats and circling about himself, his eyes golden and smoking. The last thing I saw before giving in to the dark was him fixing those terrible eyes upon me. Weakly, I held up the pouch with the root in my right hand and dropped into blackness.

I woke to the sound of fire. I sat up and opened my eyes to see Arthur seated across from me. I reached over to my broken arm and immediately understood.

Will you tell me your dream?

I could not tell where the break had happened. And, at once, I felt as though the fog had lifted somewhat. My name was still lost to me, but many other things were now clear. He stared at me across the fire, waiting, knowing.

"It was no dream," I said.

"No," he replied.

"And you did this," I said, touching my left arm. "You hea-"

"Yes."

We sat in silence for a time, contemplating.

"Why can't you just heal yourself?"

He grinned, having anticipated the question. "Because," he said "I've lost my true name."

I cocked my head to one side.

"And you, boy, are the only one left alive who remembers it."

It hadn't yet become completely clear, but, for the first time, I felt my feet upon the path. We sat again for a few moments, thinking, planning. I broke the silence.

"What will you do wi-"

"Mend the world," he said. "With my true name, I will mend the world." Then, "And myself."

It did not feel like the truth; certainly not the whole of it. But, knowing now that my dreams weren't dreams at all but memories…

"What's my name?"

"I cannot say."

"Cannot say or do not kn-"

"It would kill me, your name," he said."

I gritted my teeth. "Do you have any straight answers? Or just riddles."

He grunted. "The only straight answers ARE riddles, boy."

I rolled my eyes.

A noise came from the depths of the dark, sounding only once. He stood, alert, but his hands stayed from his hilt. I stood with him, and cast my eyes all about us in search of the wolf. His gaze never faltered. It wasn't long before we were both staring into the inky black, though I'm sure he saw more than I, that he knew what it was without seeing it.

"We leave here before first light," he said, and immediately began preparing for bed.

I stared into the dark for a moment longer, contemplating the wolf.

Across the Map

We were out of food and food had become hard to find. The landscape hadn't changed much, but, as we moved ever westward, the rustle and scurry sounds of animals in the underbrush became increasingly rare. Arthur had noticed but made no mention of it, aside from a solitary "Fuck!" which punctuated the end of an overlong and fruitless hunt.

I noticed him looking over his shoulder and squinting into the distance, less self-conscious, more concerned . After the first few days, he began to increase our pace. Little by little, we spent less time resting and more time traveling. Some mornings, we'd start off before dawn had announced herself, roused and making tracks upon the muddy fog-blurred hem of the morning, our bellies sour and hollow. Before long, he had us moving for two and three days at a time, navigating thorns, stumbling over stones and into holes. It wasn't long after that before I lost track of how long we had been traveling. Everything melded together in this mysterious panicked rush. He hardly spoke. I stopped asking questions. We rode on. Hungry. Thinning.

Eventually, we came to a weather beaten sign that read "Halverson's Seat". The lettering was tall and faded, but rendered in elegant script. Most of the paint had long since flaked away; the old wooden sign was now leaning to the left, sunken in the morass and obscured by overgrowth.

I might not have noticed it at all had he not stopped to look at it.

He sat atop his horse for a moment, staring at the sign in silence. Then, he dismounted and walked directly up to the sign. After examining it closely for another few moments, he raised a hand of crooked fingers and chanted something under his breath. Something in the sign subtly flickered to life, a soft golden light outlining a series of lines and various other shapes. Underlying it all was a spiral; a spiral of thorns, it seemed. I could hardly tell from where I was and reasoned that was why Arthur had dismounted to get a closer look. But Arthur kept staring at the sign as if waiting for it to come to life.

He turned toward me and raised an eyebrow when he saw the puzzled look on my face. "Tell me what you see, boy."

"I see a map?" I guessed. "There are a lot of lines and a I can't quite s-"

He strode toward me with sudden purpose and I was once again surprised at how quickly he could move with the right motivation. Without a word, he commanded me from the back of the horse and led me by his stare to stand before the sign.

"Now?" he said.

We both looked again, though I was certain now that he couldn't see it... whatever it was. But being closer did not clarify the image at all. It lay just beneath the letters and symbols, a tangle of lines traced in subtle golden light. It seemed a spiral of thorns. I turned to face him and saw his brow was furrowed as if he was hung on some diabolical riddle. The tip of his tongue was poked out of the corner of his mouth, a tiny pink thing suspended in a great tangle of beard.

It would seem that he needed me in more ways than he had initially let on. And whatever obscene need had motivated him to place his trust in a strange caged child was the same thing motivating him to keep me alive. As we were closing in on resolving that motivation, I thought it best to prove myself useful sooner than later. So I held back a childish lie to preserve myself.

"I think it's a map."

"You think?"

"It's hard to tell. I can see enough to know that something is there, but everytime I try to fix my eyes on it, it fades to almost nothing. It's... spinning... without moving."

He grunted, frustrated. Tired. Like he had done this many times before and that this was always the outcome. "We?" I thought, as he leaned over my shoulder and spoke into my ear.

"Repeat after me," he said. "-

It is an ocean composed of oceans. you cannot hope to contain it. You cannot control it. In time, however, you may become skilled enough to enter the waters without drowning. And, then, You must allow the pain to bring you to full demonstration, to full knowledge. You are not only pain, but it is the pain you avoid, the pain you cloak. Be still in the fullness of your existence and know yourself.

The memory came in a vivid flash and faded just as dramatically, leaving only a single word behind. I did not hear him and did not repeat him.

Nevertheless, the subtle tangle of golden lines unwound themselves and became much more legible. I studied the map for a moment before turning and pointing.

"That way takes us to Halverson's Seat," I offered. "Is that where we-"

Arthur was staring at me again. "It came back to you, didn't it?" He smirked beneath his beard. "Speak aloud her name and reveal the path to us."

I blushed. "I only repeated after you."

"Indeed," he said. "Only I didn't utter a word."

The Multitude

He called it a name I cannot pronounce and told me it was "Coven-Sign". I didn't know exactly what he'd meant but gathered from the look and sound of him that coven-sign was a worrying prospect, whatever the whole meaning.

We bedded down as usual; far off road and nestled against the dark - no fire. He rummunated longer than normal before finally falling asleep, his riddles dissolving at long last into gentle troubled snoring. I fell asleep shortly afterward, thinking of coven-sign, thinking of the way he had said, "Your wolf."

Morning came with a new quietness that woke me bolt upright.

There was no snoring. He was gone.

I looked all around where he'd been sleeping and checked the horses - two picked at the grasses right where we'd tied them the night before. I thought that he might be getting sick again and strained to listen for the telltale sound of it.

Instead, I heard laughing.

At first, it was just a tiny whisper of a thing, the end bits of something greater. But as I began to walk in its direction, it became clearer - much clearer, in fact. It was as if it had always been this loud and we hadn't taken notice.

All questions of why we would not have taken notice vanished in a waterfall of laughter. I could not help it. I laughed along.

As I crested a hill while following the ever increasing sound of children's laughter, I was surprised (and, yet, not at all surprised) to see a child running past me, tilting this way and that, turning cartwheels and flips of all sorts. The child was quickly joined by another. And then another. And then so many others.

I continued to laugh, and began running with them.

The remarkable thing was how well they were kept - for all their tossing and leaping, there wasn't a stray strand to be found on their clothing, nor a mark on their bodies. "Where were their parents?" I wondered absently, now being tossed, spinning, looping, landing, and in stride.

There came, still, more children.

We, now a great undulating swell of laughing, tumbled unexpectedly into a neatly appointed town square. Upon noticing the change in surroundings, I immediately ceased laughing and began to look around, slowing from the maniac-child pace to hardly walking at all.

It was then that it all filled itself in.

As I stared into the first of the buildings, I began wondering what might be inside; perhaps a bakery? No sooner did I have that thought than the very thing began to appear before my eyes, and then was there - truly there - and hadn't it always been?

It becomes difficult to say what one is looking at, when it is always what you think you are seeing (or should be seeing?).

This was the look of the place; a dozen buildings formed an outer circle around 9 other larger buildings which themselves encircled three very tall, beautifully domed towers. Just beyond this circular square, a great number of buildings had been carved into the adjacent hillside. A river lay between and curved around these, tumbling somehow gracefully downhill, before running straight and clear, just beyond the edge of the square, the sun glinting powerfully off its surface.

The children, once a laughing tumbling mess, were still pleasant, but now… solemn? The word escapes me. I turned about as the children filed past me, suddenly orderly, suddenly silent, and I felt a thinness to this truth.

I wondered how we could have missed such a thing, and had I been running that long, and wh-

-ed to get something to eat. Most of the children seemed to have departed (gone home, I thought) and the remaining few were directing me toward the bakery. "Sweets?" I thought but, by now, knew, and there they were! Once inside, the laughing began again in full force and I was immediately taken by it. We gorged ourselves on cakes, tarts, pies, all incoming at a nearly forced rate, all while laughing, and why are we laughing? And what's in th-

-erd and I said thank you and lay down on the floor beside the woodstove. I felt one last thing kick inside me before I drifted off to sleep on a full belly. A nonsense thing. A single word.

Run.

I let it kick itself out before surrendering to the warmth around me, burying myself in the ample quilt and tunneling downward into sleep.

Interlude: Reception

Shadrach was surprised he hadn't confronted him sooner.

He had become restless watching. For this entire watch, Shadrach had been ignoring the pull of his instincts and was now beginning to feel the ache of the strain. As time wore on, he found himself attending less and pretending more, imagining the sweetness of Arthur's blood in his mouth, the stink of the old man's corpse finally beneath his paws.

Shadrach knew where those thoughts would lead him, yet he found himself being led with decreasing resistance. Being led by them gave him something other than the promise of guilt to stand upon. These thoughts foreshadowed justice finally done, not a cruelty, not a bloody betrayal.

"Watch," he had been told. "See that no harm comes to him."

Hunting would not help this time. Yet, hunting was all he wanted to do.

As they drew closer to their goal, wildlife became increasingly sparse. The trees and grasses grew thick and wild, but, after a while, not so much as a sparrow tittered amidst the leaves.

When the presence of animals began to fade to nothing, Shadrach allowed the pair to drift further and further from him, lingering behind to eat what he could, to hunt, before sprinting by night to catch up to them while they slept.

Tonight, he had been sloppy.

He was miles off when he came across their scent. He sat, panting with the effort, allowing a single plaintive whine to escape before wrigging himself, head to tail, and proceeding. By the time he came upon them, his breathing had returned to normal.

Seeing them, he laid down and watched as they prepared to do the same. He was hungry and felt his mind begin to drift. To him, it seemed a momentary indiscretion. He was wrong.

"I should have guessed she would send her mongrel to negotiate."

Even knowing it was too late, Shadrach's eyes flew open, his muscles flexing to the ready. The old man had found him, but stood several feet off, waiting.

"Time is short," Shadrach said patiently. "You know why I am here."

"Turn 'round.

Shadrach stood, aware of a growl rising within himself. They both stood staring at one another, evaluating, discerning, assessing. The old man balanced himself on wobbling legs, a knotted hand hovering over the hilt of his sword.

"Surely, she wouldn't mind having you back home. 'Stead of out here. Alone." He smirked slightly. "Couldn't be that she's afraid of a sick old man, could it? The Gr-"

"Release him to me and you'll live."

"He has been released and has given his word."

"Maybe," Shadrach said, relaxing outwardly. He cast a quick glance toward the boy and saw that he had not moved. "But he was never yours to take. And this folly, this farce you've summoned him to hel-"

"Tell your master that I'd prefer to be threatened in person. Then go. That's how this ends. That is also the only way you survive this."

"Mistress, not master, is the preferred nomenclature. And I gather you're beginning to realize that you are indeed being threatened in person."

Arthur bristled, but only for a moment. "You know why I do this."

"Yes."

"And... you know what this is," he said, tapping his scabbard.

Shadrach snorted.

Arthur continued, "I could have you on the end of this. Could have several times by now; I did not need to wait for you to wake. Broth-"

"We are NOT brothers." Shadrach spat.

Arthur drew the blade, transforming before Shadrach's eyes. "If that's the way it's go-"

Having already surrendered to his basest instincts, Shadrach leapt forward with the fullness of his strength and speed.

Arthur charged to meet him.

The Memory

When the voice called out to him, He knew it was false. He could hear the wrong in it, the subtle ways in which the mimicry failed. He thought, perhaps, he might be able to devise the thing that actually called to him. Yet... it was close - so very close to the real thing. And it had been so long since anything - even memory - had come close to anything like the real thing. And he was weak.

But, mostly, he was tired.

Grieving wasn't a thing he ever learned to do and falling in love (he would learn afterward) was a thing no man who did not know grief (and, having known it, survived it) could feel sincerely. But he had felt it sincerely, and pledged himself to her. She did the least she could to acknowledge him, and withheld her name. It would be months before she told him, and every day of that waiting was somehow sweeter.

The last time he heard her name was from his own mouth. Screaming. Helpless.

Useless.

The years in between her death and his now, the wasted hours scouring mountainsides and caves and treetops and shorelines for demons - he saw the waste of it all now, the misspending of her memory, the loss of his purpose, the void of meaning.

"What can this mean but that she might have me one more time?" he thought. The madness did not escape him, nor he it; grinning weakly, he cast a glance at the sleeping boy. And, just as he was satisfied the boy would not wake, he cast his gambit.

Rising noiselessly was not an easy feat, much less walking, much less both in his body. He rose carefully and clumsily, as one drunk, and nearly gave the game away with a clatter of his scabbard. There was a moment where he heard himself protest, but then the phantom sounded.

"This is death," he thought. "And how many are bid so sweetly to their end?"

Resigned to obey, he began walking slowly, resolving, at first, to stay within earshot of the boy. Yet, as he neared it, the voice seemed to correct itself to memory, to fill itself out with more truth. He knew this to be a part of the illusion, but he followed anyway, praying, promising, failing.

And, then, as smooth and welcome as cool water, her hand was upon him, her arm around him, their hand joined. And they danced, upward, outward, into the furthest parts of the night.

Some part of him thought that he had given up long ago, that this fault was willful, that he deserved, at least, this He tried to summon the feeling of purpose that once drove him and then her voice sounded, calling his name all the clearer, and he took another step.

He remembered his promise to her, knowing that this could not be less of what she wanted. He remembered her eyes, the sheen on her hair, and remembered being tangled. He felt his destiny - his duty - and yet… she was here. Looking into her eyes, even false ones, he no less felt the truth of her spirit ring out within him, once and loud, a single word.

"Run."

The patience in her voice was unmistakable. He remembered the curve from her wrist, down her hand, to the end of her little finger. He thought she might have been remembered better. Yet, the phantom sounded and he took another step.

"It's like dancing," he thought, and was taken.

Convensign

He thought that he wouldn't have paid enough attention to it the first time had it not been for his need to make sure that the boy could see the covensign also - the subtly illuminated fractal repetition etched upon the aging wood; a marker, a summoning seal, an claim of sorts. It was, at least, a simple sign; lines undulating outward, steepled at their intersections. But there were eight lines, meaning eight generations of coven had survived and entrenched themselves here. Hundreds of them, at least, had lived here, thriving unchallenged, unmolested, growing stronger, attracting others, sharing knowledge.

Eight generations.

He heard again, speaking his name with her voice, this time spoken directly into his ear. He curled his face toward her, and felt the strength of her lure - he did not have long before succumbing would be removed as an option. Nevertheless, he could not without himself from returned her name as a floating whisper, a shameful need, a prayer:

"Nayota. My Beloved."

In spite of the consistent and steadily increasing pull from within and without, an instinct shook himself from the thinness of the illusion and back toward recollection.Yet, again, he heard her voice, his name, stronger now, sweeter now. But, again, he heard the wrongness in it, the unfamiliarity. She was the shape and the sound, but the soul was vacant. This thing that held her could never represent her, not even as this alluring apparition.

He'd eyed the boy hard enough that the young man dismounted wordlessly and had come to get a better look at the sign. But, when the boy was finally standing directly before it, the old man thought he had seen a flash in the young man's eyes, the vaguest of calculations. It might have been the preparation of a lie. The old man had taken note, and had leaned into the boy's ear to whisper.

"Repeat after me," he'd begun, and, for a moment, had felt his nose brush against the boy's earlobe. He had recoiled, as one stung, watching the boy struggle with the fragment of memory he'd mistakenly triggered. He thought he might know what the boy was thinking, but starred and then asked plainly if he had recalled a memory.

The boy lied and Arthur smirked beneath his beard, knowing and knowing why.

"I only repeated after you," the boy had said.

"Indeed," he had said, both of them now knowing the lie.

Now, as her arms stretched and encircled him, he felt something in that embrace that raised tacit. Something in that grasp was more tentacle than tender.

He met her eyes again and, in spite of his fear, despite his instincts' insistence of danger, he was, nevertheless, undone.

From all he could tell, it may have been her voice that brought him back from that brink. "Poison," he thought and felt. Her arms held him closer, tighter.

...they will say, "it's only wolfsong", to distract from the fact that a pack of fanged...

He snapped back to recollection. Still dancing, still soaring, still in her arms but more aware.

He felt the poison eat him away from the inside, felt the larger hidden part of the it-that-wasn't-her feeding upon him, and felt a kind of grief. He remembered with caustic clarity, mourning her, burying her, surviving the many long and empty hours without her. He remembered that criminal feeling of subtraction, of unearned and unexplained loss.

This could not be her.

He briefly wondered what manner of creature had finally grabbed him, what monstrous horror had persevered where so many others had failed and fallen, before he began sliding his left hand, slowly, carefully, up her back toward the base of her neck. She leaned into his touch, and they rose together.

#

A single witch presents no problem on their own. Usually, he found, they were simply lovers of nature - a bit overtaken and strange (in his opinion) but that didn't make them dangerous. At the most, a witch - even an exceedingly ill-tempered witch, may curse or hex you - certainly not a thing you wanted, to be sure, but nothing life threatening. He'd found that, largely, witches attended to their own affairs, and, when pressed or otherwise persuaded, they dabbled in affairs of the realm about them, before returning to the secrets of their mushrooms and moon rites.

An entire coven was quite another matter altogether.

Witches, while decidedly polite, were fiercely solitary, and, as such, almost never interacted with anyone. Therefore, witches were best left as they were to do as they pleased. Yet there were a few circumstances and pursuations compelling enough to entice witches to gather, to discuss, to plan, and, in the rarest of circumstances, to collaborate.

It would have begun as a conclave. where covens gathered others eventually followed. He had counted eight generations, but was already doubting his eyes; it could not be that many. Not in one place. Not entirely unknown. Distantly, he wondered how long they had been gathered here.

He reread the covensign, and then reread it again even more closely; eight generations - there would be thousands of them. And, given the nearby presence of Ogmwa they would have gone undisturbed for those eight generations.

He thought of their sheer number, and an unfamiliar rigid cold worked its way through him.

Overcoming and/or persuading a village would have been easy; easier, at least. Taking on an untold number of witches all primed for their arrival was an entirely different matter. Not for the first time, he felt himself sink slightly under the weight of the task before them.

...only wolfsong, my beloved...

He smiled at the thought of her, her quality, and found strength. He'd made peace long ago that he was not doing this for her, but that she was, nonetheless, with him. And it was all the more difficult to deny this feeling, this togetherness, now that he was dancing in her arms again.

They spun up and through the air a final time, hips parallel, her spectral eyes upon him.

He did not bid it farewell.

Once his right hand gripped the hilt of his sword, the illusion collapsed at once and in total. It cried out, the thing still feeding upon him and, likely, not at all pleased to have been discovered. He took enough time to see that it had sank several of its fanged tentacles into his sides, puppeting him whilst draining him dry during the dance. Before he had fully grasped what it was that had him, he struck out with lightning speed, slashing at the creature multiple times, severing the siphoning tentacles, and falling to the earth.

He slashed, stabbed, tearing deep wounds, sliding down the main trunk of the creature - a tower of forked and mouthed tentacles - slowing his descent with his sword while parting the creature from itself.

It tried her name again but was it much too broken now. And he had seen; he could no longer allow the farce.

Later, standing over the corpse, he still could not say for sure what it had been; even in its clearest form, he may not have known it. Visually, he examined his wounds, swinging his sword once, hard and away from himself, repelling the poisoned gore to the ground. He looked for the last time before-

The boy.

There was a brief moment where he oriented himself before departing in a great burst of light.

The Slaughter

We lay by the fire within an arm's length of one another, yet did not speak. Occasionally, the old man would nod off and begin snoring, a resonant growl that rose and fell with his breathing. He lay on his side against the bare earth with his back to the fire with one large arm curled about himself. The other arm lay along his side with its hand hovering just beyond the reach of the sword.

The purring would last only until some small interruption disturbed it; a pop from the fire, the hoot of an owl, or the vigorous rustling of some unknown thing. At that, he'd spring to life, his eyes flying open, searching, his breath held in his throat.

The first few times, I leapt awake with him, and, for a moment or two, we were as we had been during our first encounter with the wolf. But after several starts with no wolf, I became less fearful, less eager to leap to my own defense. Before long, I had fallen into a shallow sleep.

I awoke just as dawn began to break to see him still on watch. He sat with his back to the fire, his knees drawn up to his chest, his scabbard resting atop them. I wondered if he had been sick throughout the night or, perhaps, this morning as I rested. The tenuous truce struck the previous night had not made us any less suspicious of one another, yet I could not help but feel a pang of sympathy for him.

He became aware of my gaze and shook himself into full awareness before standing and walking off toward the horses. I gathered myself and stood. yawning loudly and stretching my limbs as far as they would go.

Before long, he came to me with a bundle in his hands and handed it to me. It was a filthy shirt, pants, and a mismatched pair of boots. The shirt and pants were both torn and stained in places with splotches of dark red-brown. I knew what it was, but would not allow myself to imagine it.

I took the bundle from his hand and pretended not to notice the stains, not to care about it or even know what it was, but it was no use. I thought that something in my face or actions must have betrayed my thoughts, until I noticed where his gaze was fixed.

He himself had noticed the blood, and was visibly moved by the sight of it. His eyes never left the clothing until I had taken it from his hand and afterward, he refused to meet my gaze.

"If he has any shame in him," I thought, "you're seeing it now."

The stains on the clothing begged a number of questions, all the more as after I had unbundled the items and saw the clothing was sized for a child - a child very near to my own size. Fear came and went, a flash of summer lightning; I knew then that childhood would not insulate me from harm. Yet I rose to meet that fear, feeling a certain defiant strength coursing through me. I denied him a reaction, dressing without a word. I put the shirt on last of all, pulling it over my head and pushing my arms through the sleeves.

He looked at my then, openly considering the bloodstains, as if to make sure that I would take notice of them.

"Suits you," he said.

"It itches," I said.

At that, he turned and started off toward the last living horse.

#

I had awoken that morning to the memory of my father. He appeared clearly to me and known. Knowing him began as a kind of shock that immediately settled into a quieting certainty. He was here. And known.

I was saved.

As I drew breath to call his name, I watched in horror as he was split in two by a blinding streak of light and obliterated. The last thing I saw was his face. Afterward, there was only light. The other children around me awoke and began to scream, fleeing in all directions. The light remained and continued its work.

It slashed and parted everything, splitting arms from shoulders, heads from necks. With each slash, the screaming got louder. Yet, there was something in this that felt like truth. I thought the light might be a dream, a foretelling. Even with the screams of bloodied children dominating the atmosphere, I could already feel my horror begin to grapple with something like relief.

I knew that the light had come for me.

I stood, the horror yet retreating from my heart, and walked toward it. But, after a step or two, I felt myself withheld by the wrist. "Both wrists," it occurred to me. The strangeness of the realization also held me, and I turned to look to each wrist.

I saw a child upon each of my wrists, latched there with overly white teeth, gnawing and slurping between punctuations of screaming. Even this did not wake me. I thought, "They are children, like me," but could feel they were not, could feel the not-children's teeth digging ever deeper into my wrists.

Not. Children.

I looked up again toward the light just in time to see it cleave through all the children about me, each taken by the light in a swift slash before falling to the ground in parts. Then the light was all around me, and was everything.

Then I fell asleep.

I could feel time pass, yet all was still. Even me. Even my thoughts were void.

And then it was and ever had been him, Arthur, his filthy fingers down my throat as, eyes watering, I emptied my belly onto the ground.

I looked at what I had eaten with great delight the night before, a gummy puddle of hairs and parts, covered in pale white mucus. I had nothing left to give, yet I tried.

I thought Arthur might rush to have me stand, to punish me. Seeing the mess, even as it was for the first time, was not. A part of me had seen it, and eaten anyway.

I remembered every moment as pure bliss. I remembered when the light came for me. And, now, thinking quietly between each noisy evacuation, I could see why it was that Arthur spoke in riddles.

I felt his hand against my neck and became aware of him in a different way. I looked up from the mess and into his eyes. He smiled weakly, before closing his eyes with a sigh.

It all came at once.

The first thing I noticed was him; knowing him and the how and the why - I saw him absolutely perfectly from beginning to end. And then the rest came, a calamity of voices, face after face until they were all him, and all of them were him, the perfect image of him splintered into countless fragments. He housed, it seemed, too many memories for one man.

I felt the truth of what I said before the meaning had become clear to me. I became aware that I had also closed my eyes, and opened them to see him weeping, silent.

Knowing that I would lose even this fractured clarity one he removed his hand, I summoned the strength to speak.

"They've taken your name," I said.

He opened his eyes and offered a struggling grin. "They did."

He dropped his hand from my neck and the vastness vanished like steam. I could not hold on to much more than the memory of my own words, but it was enough to get to the truth.

I thought long before finally speaking. "Are we called the same?"

He stood, wiping his face. "You ask me?! After all that you saw..." he said, trailing off and busying himself building a fire.

"All that I saw," I thought but did not say.

I let him continue building the fire.

All that you saw...

A long and thoughtful silence passed between us as the newly summoned fire crackled nearby.

I heard a snort come from where the horses had last been tied and saw only one. I remembered the mess I'd wretched up. I remembered the smell of the bakery, the kindness of the children. And I remembered the marvel of the destructive light that came to find me.

Collecting myself, I stood, and walked toward him. He was sat down against a tree, eyes cast downward. He did not look up when I reached him.

"I don't think mine are dreams," I said.

"Neither are mine," he said. "But what else would you call them?"

I paused a final time before offering. I thought of what I saw, where we might be jaded and what he might be using me to accomplish. He was right; "All I saw" and I couldn't see the emptiness that came with it. I couldn't see, even seeing him perfectly, that he had been stripped of something vital. What dreams I did have were fleeting and scattered. But, surely, there was one I could hold onto long enough to speak aloud.

I offered to try. He accepted. I hesitated, looking about me with well earned trepidation. He saw me, and he drew slightly closer.

"I withheld too much from you," he began again. "I am less able than I believed. And, now, we are caught in this. Because of me."

Blind

"Ogmwa!"

The voice rang out in the darkness, echoing off the damp walls of the cave.

"Ogmwa! Gana-Briel, Blind Eater of –"

There was a rumbling then, followed by an unbearable stench. A low graveled growl came up from the depths of the cave. The owner of the voice ventured further into the cave, dragging a burlap sack behind him. After a short distance, the voice began once more, less sure of itself. "Ogmwa! Gana-Bri –"

"Ogmwa, Blind Eater of Gana Brielle, Defiler of Orsik…. Yes. It know its own names." The voice came with sudden power, dark, ancient, resonating forcely, at once preposterously abundant yet infinitely hollow. Danforth had not ever heard anything like it.

"And It knows who calls to it now. It knows very well, Danforth, son of Ryan, son of Drake, son of Eustice, son of Marlo, son of Articald, son of Morg–"

"Enough!", Danforth cried, his voice trembling. He felt a wild sort of fear begin to creep up inside himself and knew that he would have to act quickly" I am here to make a deal."

"It does not… deal, Danforth human." Ogmwa spat out the last word like a curse. "But you knew this. And, knowing this, you've still come. This can only end o-"

"You know why I've come, Eater. I had no choice." Danforth fumbled with the ties at the top of the wriggling sack he'd brought with him. A tiny whimper escaped the sack. Danforth's demeanor remained unchanged.

"And you've brought it... a gift?!"

"I have come prepared to deal."

There was a long period of silence. Danforth opened his mouth to ask again when Ogmwa replied.

"You seek the blessed vessel of Ryan Cross, sacred instrument of the once mighty and numerous Blades of True Rest... it is your father's sword, his memory. his... human soul."

The walls, ceiling and floor, seemed to shift slightly. Danforth took notice and gritted his teeth.

"That is why you have come. Confess it."

"Yes," replied I must –"

"You must convince me. And survive me; that is the sum of your obligations."

"I! Must! Have it!" Danforth's declaration fell dead against the thick wetness of the way around.

For a while, no further sounds came from the depths of the cave. Danforth strained his eyes, trying in vain to overcome the darkness. Aftera great while, Ogmwa spoke again.

"Present your... offering."

With great haste, Danforth knelt beside the sack he'd dragged with him. After a few seconds of struggle with a knot, he gave in to frustration and nerves, producing a dagger to cut the cords holding the sack closed. . With both hands, he reached inside and pulled out a small boy. His hands and feet were bound, his eyes open and wild, yet seeing nothing; they were not yet used to the flat dark of the cave.

"Dead", Ogmwa said flatly. "No deal."

Danforth sawed away at the boy's bonds, sweating profusely, his hands trembling. "His heart still beats!" he cried. "Listen, Eater. I know you can hear it."

There was silence from the depths. Then, "Yes. It lives. Present your offering."

"How long has it been since you've fed, Eater. How long have you hungered here, alone in the –"

"It is not alone."

For a moment, Danforth contemplated what that might mean. And, though his better instincts bid him to consider it further, Ogmwa interrupted.

"Six hundred twenty-two days," it said. "It hungers greatly."

"Then that is the bargain; relinquish the sword and I'll-"

"Present your offering," came the voice from the depths. "I am not one of your gods, and I will not ask another time."

Danforth severed the last of the boy's bonds and slapped her awake. "Up, child! Up, damn you!"

The boy stirred and blinked. Two white eyes peered out from his dirty tear streaked face. Danforth wasted no time inspiring the child toward the dark.

"Quickly, boy!" he cried. Pointing toward the depths of the cave, he shouted.

"Your parents! Run!"

The boy, confused and disoriented, nevertheless hesitated only a moment before fleeing deeper into the cave. "Mother!", he cried. "Father! I'm lost! Mother can you hear me? Where are –"

The sound of his footsteps which had been receding with regular splash-stomp intervals, stopped suddenly after a few dozen steps. There was a groaning, a wet sound of many lashes reaching out and finding purchase, and, finally, a childish grunt that receded into the dark and became silence.

Danforth waited in the inky black, holding his breath. Eventually, the create spoke

"He was young, Danforth. Very young. Have you no pity?"

"The sword," said Danforth.

"Does not Danforth have a child of his own? A young boy? Like this one?"

Ogmwa grumbled from the depths. "Yes," he continued. "A son. It can see him. It can see him very well."

Danforth swallowed hard. "The sword, monster" he commanded. "Now."

"Too young," said Ogmwa. "He would have been... much sweeter... later on."

Danforth's fear was spiked to its apex. He retreated to what he knew best - bravado. "I've honored our arrangement. Now it's your turn."

There was another terrible rumbling churning sound, much louder than the first. Then, silence. Ogmwa spoke again, seemingly satisfied.

"Come forth and claim what you have earned."

Danforth hesitated a moment, the peak of his fear birthing sparks of paranoia. But it was not enough. Swallowing his instincts, he forced himself to venture further into the darkness, swiveling his head about himself blindly, foolishly, his arms out like great feelers in the thickness of the infinite dark. The further he tred, the warmer it became. It wasn't long at all before he was gagging audibly from the smell.

"The child, Danforth... It would have not believed it, had It not seen it with its own eyes. Had It not... "

Danforth took a single step backward, and waited. Almost immediately, the ground seemed to incline downward. Casting his eyes toward what he believed to be the direction of entrance, Danforth saw no sign of light.

"Further human." The voice was all around him now, smothering him. He pressed the folds of his cloak against his mouth and continued on.

The ground beneath him had changed. What was once firm stone had become soft and muddy. The smell was oppressive. Still, he labored forward. A terrible gurgling sound came from all around him, many times louder than before. His legs began to tingle. He looked down at his feet in vain. The blackness was impenetrable. The smell seemed an all consuming stench.

"Do you know the meaning of my name, Danforth? It was given me by the daughter of Lord Itamar, a gift she granted It for sparing her life."

Danforth was now thigh-deep in a soft, muddy substance, his legs now tingling madly. For the first time, he thought of retreating, but found it impossible to proceed; forward or backward. He began to prepare a second attempt at a bargain.

"It is a clever name, Gana Brielle," came Ogmwa, almost painful with the force and depth of Its voice.

"The first name "Gana", an ancient word meaning "warrior". Danforth turned to retreat but found his legs unresponsive. His bargaining prowess abandoned him as the reality of his circumstances slowly became tangible.

"The second name, also ancient, has a different meaning, a better truer meaning - 'hunting ground.'"

Danforth reached down to free his legs from the muck. The instant his hands touched the muddy substance, they began to tingle. There was a feeling of "too late" that echoed within him. Twice. He remembered, then, the full tale of the monster in whose belly he was now trapped.

He thought about the boy he'd cut free had died. He wondered if anything died in here at all. By then, his legs had given out, his hips as well. He sunk into the muck, neither screaming nor protesting, regardless of the protest of his feral heart. "Wait," he thought. You will find the answer."

"Gana Brielle can be interpreted to mean "Warrior Hunting Ground. But not in the sense that you might suppose. Warriors do not come here to hunt."

The truth had already been realized, but Danforth cursed It anyway. "You... monster."

"They come here... and are hunted."

The cave pulsed and throbbed around him. He could feel it now - the walls, the ceiling, and floor all vibrated with singular life and vitality. And had they always been so alive? So animated? He felt himself, suddenly, tossed. Churned.

The flesh fell from Danforth's hand. He struggled against the muck, desperate, screaming, his soon tongue muted, his mind a furious storm of second chances.

"Be still, human. You are... upsetting me," came Ogmwa. And now the voice.

He understood why the sword he sought remained there, why they all did. He thought, even then, in his final moments, that he might better understand. He wished and could not say what he wished. His head was yet above the much and, even with all his planning, all his careful considerations, that this would end in doom.

As Danforth heard the gurgling sound a final time, he thought of the boy he had sacrificed. Real tears came then, though they were selfish. The best of him came forth at the worst time, and he saw with unrelenting clarity the evil he had wrought on his way here, to this cave, to this mouth, to his death.

"He's eating me," he thought, even feeling his face sink slowly beneath the muck, the lower half becoming it. "He's eating me alive."

His eyes sat just above the line of digestive gunk he found himself tossed and turned in, actively consumed. And, he thought, he had bargained well. And fairly.

He did not see it, but felt the blade as it punched through his sternum. For a moment, he could see his father. He could see them all. Even in this horror, he was moved by the image of his ancestors.

"They only come to feed me," Ogmwa spoke, satisfied, even with Danforth struggling weakly, fruitlessly. "They only come for one reason."

Danforth thought he might draw upon some forgotten lore that would free him in this final moment. He remembered the stories he had been told, the legends from which he'd descended. He thought he might survive this, and summoned his full might to rise to his feet.

"I am..." he screamed at last before becoming a swallowed thing.

The deed done, Ogmwa loosed his tethers to the opening of the cave, tendrils laden with tacky chunks of the partially digested.

Bait.

Not for the first time, he wondered why they continued to come.

"Because they still believe," he thought and did not understand.

The mouth of the cave saw a bluster of gaseous emissions before settling back to a quiet inconspicuous thing.

He found himself wondering what they believed and could not devine an answer. It did not matter. There was only waiting.

He drifted but did not slumber.

Talmek The Seer

He ran his right hand through his hair and stared at the sky a moment, contemplating, remembering.

"I have withheld too much from you," he began. It sounded like an apology. I did not reply.

"I'll tell you all that I am able to tell. But what I know amounts to broken pieces. I can only tell you so much and only in my way. Y'understand?"

"Yes."

He pulled a pipe from his pocket and began the work of cleaning it and packing it with fresh tobacco, but his mind was elsewhere, his brow creased with concern. After fiddling with the pipe for a few moments, he began to speak.

"The creature to the North is a child of Ibsis," he began, "the plague that rots the world and all that lives therein. I have followed it here to the abandoned kingdom of Orsik, to this village, and, now to the cave called 'Gana Brielle'.

"A child of wha-"

"'It' used to be called 'Talmek'; Talmek the Seer.

Something unfamiliar shifted within me in response to that name. I kept it to myself for want of a way to properly describe it. I thought yet again of the pies and the cakes and the gore that followed. This time, the shifting came with a gurgling in my stomach. I thought I might have felt something move. But it was too subtle. It was nerves. I ignored my bubbling guts, eager to listen.

"According to the common men, Talmek was a wise and powerful alchemist and astronomer, in addition to being a gifted Oracle. And, while impressing common folk was an achievement in itself, those in the High City of Orsik held no such regard. His fame extended only to the borders of his village and no further. So when he entered the High City and had the audacity to request an audience with the king…"

He trailed off tapping the pipe a few times against the heel of his right hand.

I leaned forward, interested. "Why was he so determined to speak with His Majesty?"

The old man was still busying himself with his pipe, fidgeting, blowing into the stem and holding it up to his eye. Only when he was satisfied that the stem was cleared, did he continue. "He wished to warn His Majesty. Talmek had had a vision of The Myriad - a cataclysm that was to be the end of everything.

"If he were going to warn him, he must have known what to do to prevent it, no?" I asked.

He cast a glance at me, visibly miffed by my interruption. "Patience, boy." I nodded sheepishly.

"The first time, Talmek told them what was to come. And he spoke true - we are, all of us, living in the truth of the prophecy rendered. But then, the world had not yet seen nor felt anything of the kind he described. They kept him there long enough to finish before laughing him out. The second time, he came with villagers as witnesses. They were, Talmek and his cohorts, certain that this could not be overlooked.

"Right was on their side - truth, in their eyes. It seemed to them, a clear conclusion - a plague was coming, and they must prepare. But, as some say, wine and comfort cloud the whole truth. And the company of the king, sat high in padded chairs and deep into their cups, would only abide this dour intrusion for so long. It did not take long before the audience was forced to an early end. Leaping from his seat, Bruce grabbed Talmak and dragged him by the throat into the depths of the dungeon as the king's court drowned out Talmek's supplications with raucous laughter and harmonious ridicule. The rest, believers that they were in Talmek, were run out of the castle by those same drunkards with swords, guffawing and falling over themselves the whole time, running a few of them through for good measure.

He sighed. "Good measure." The fire popped and caught his attention immediately, only this time, I noticed his hand did not shoot to his hilt. I looked about us and wondered if the wolf still lingered. I looked at him and it seemed from his demeanor it might not be so. He spoke on.

"Talmak was released the next morning with the strictest of warnings that they should never return.

"Nevertheless, Talmek resolved to return a third time. Before this, some say, he consorted with and was eventually seduced by those who would offer false promises, temporary glimmers, bated truths, all while using the power Talmak wielded for their own contrary ends."

Arthur pinched a measure, packed the bowl, and lit it, drawing slowly and deeply before exhaling a lazy lingering . He looked at the boy and gently snorted a vapor tumbling gently in his direction.

I sneezed and felt my stomach harden against it ahead of my effort. Then a pinch. Inside me. And, just as quickly, forgotten. I sneezed again, on purpose, and did not feel anything out of the ordinary. I seated my fears in my trust of Arthur.

And, having grinned with an abundance of satisfaction due to my sneezing, he continued.

"After a season or two had passed, he came again to the gates of the king's castle, again begging an audience. He had changed - they could see the robes he now wore, the myriad marks and sigils they bore; this was no layman, no ordinary doomsayer. Still, at the behest of the king, they set the guards upon him, driving him into the streets, beating him. After that the soldiers, laughing, dragged him by his heels to the city gates.

"There, they branded him in his flesh, on his forehead, the mark of a traitor. Then, after casting his robes from him and pissing upon them, they tied him to a post, whipped him, back and front, until there was only a bloodied husk. Finally, placing the sullied robes upon his stripped and shredded hangings of flesh, they threw him out as a pile just outside the gate, leaving him to rot among the beggars and lame men.

"The beating would cost him eyes, but he would retain his sight. After that final humiliation, he crawled into the shadows and vanished, never to be seen again.

"Never seen," he began, drawing deeply once again. "But certainly heard from," he finished, and spewed a great cloud in my direction.

I did not sneeze. He seemed to take no notice and continued speaking.

"This last and most painful rejection would drive him to see this Great End converted from an avoidable catastrophe to now, our most inevitable destiny. And, having seen it so clearly, having proclaimed it to his own devastation, and having lost fear of both, he could no longer be dissuaded from sharing what he later called "the fullness of my vision" - to him, the truth - no matter the cost.

Arthur stopped, and I looked at him. He trembled, and tears were in his eyes. "He was your friend," I thought, and did not say. And now-"

"He waited patiently, purposefully. When they'd all but forgotten about him (save his worthiness for mockery in winesong), Talmek returned to them, now as a silent serpent.

"He struck out in the night, secreting his way into the thoughts and dreams of the children descended from those who'd robbed him of dignity in the king's court. He charmed these small ones with lies, simple things, wooing them in the way he was once wooed; gently and falsely, drawing on their unarticulated innermost desires, seducing them with varied emotional intoxicants. Later, the deed completed, the children, one by one, rose up in the night. Taking up knives, sticks, stones - whatever they could find, they set to blinding their sleeping mothers and fathers with the full force of unrelenting childish enthusiasm."

Arthur continued to weep silently, and I drew no attention to it - he was not done yet with the tale. I shifted in my seat, suddenly feeling as though I was in need of more space.

"It is said that a wailing, such as there had never been, went up and out from a great many houses that night. But the only ears that could hear them belonged to those who had also been blinded. In the chaos, he compelled the children to disappear into the wilderness, to follow him to this... place; Gana Brielle.

I looked around us again; he seemed to invite me to do so. I opened my eyes wide, and made as if I was seeing the whole place again for the first time. I dressed it as curiosity and wonder.

He snorted.

"The children having been evacuated, he gave the members of the court their well-earned deaths, but only in the most horrible fashion. They became, all of them, acquainted again with sight, only to be plagued with visions of monsters and terrors and all manner of demons. And all of them, each terror, were they themselves.

He swallowed hard. "Wives were slain. Brothers. Dearest Friends."

He cleared his throat, and bowed his head for a moment. I did likewise.

"Talmek cursed them such that all that they had grown to cherish was taken from them, and by their own hands."

Here, the old man paused again, closing his eyes briefly as if offering a silent prayer. I, too, closed my eyes upon the horror, yet, eyes closed, I saw the slaughter in my mind's eyes all the clearer. I opened my eyes and he continued.

"When dawn came, Talmek's charm was lifted. In the light of the new dawn, the remainder of the kingdom, court and commoner alike, men were finally able to witness the horror they had visited upon the city. Devastated, many of the soldiers took their own lives, falling on their swords. Others banished themselves to the desert of White Amber Waste for fear they might succumb to the visions again."

I licked my lips, hoping he couldn't sense my fear. "What became of Talmek? And the children he took with him?"

He swallowed. "Those were just the first of them. He would return, year after year, on the eve of the massacre, compelling children to violence and, violence done, scattering the bloodied puppets to Ghana Brielle. It wasn't long before the city of Orsik forgot the sound of children's laughter, and even mourned women with child, for it was known that any child conceived in that town would be marked. And, no matter where they were sent or taken, Talmek would come, sooner or later, and claim them."

He sighed dramatically, as if a great weight had been lifted from him. "Orsik was abandoned in short order, the entire kingdom thought to be cursed. Worst, when the plague he foretold finally came, Talmek fell victim to the very thing he'd tried to protect us from. The form he took after beating back that scourge would only reflect the evil he'd become long ago."

"He became the creature," I said.

Arthur nodded. "Some say, he developed a taste for children, fattening and eating those compelled to his cave. No doubt he still has a hunger for children," he said. He was looking directly at me then and I was ignoring him as best I could. I glanced at him from the corner of my eye and noticed the hurt in his face. At once, I remembered his promise to keep my life and was flooded with questions. He continued.

"For a while, he was known as Talmek the Cursed. These days, it is called Ogmwa."

I shivered at the mention of the creature's name. And, though fear began to creep up on me. I began to understand things in a... new way.

Dark Deeds

"The name is interpreted by most to mean "death," he said. "And I wish it were as true and simple as that. But his name comes from an old myth - a superstition, or a fable, really. Can't rightly judge the difference between them, if I'm honest." The pipe trembled in his grasp and Arthur cast his eyes toward the ground. "Some believe that there's a curse powerful enough to destroy the world - the world and everything in it. And that name, that "Ogmwa"... "

I was suddenly overcome by a great stillness and certainty. "*Ogmwa suenin rundetsun...*"

Arthur raised his head to look at me.

"Go on," I said. "Please."

Arthur stared at me, for a moment longer. "That name is part of the curse. Means destroyer or something. I don't remem-"

"That which is fated to unmake the world," I spat out the words like poison.

Arthur leaned his head to the side. "Sure. Right. That's it." He swallowed hard and ran a hand over his mouth.

Inside

I awoke sore and confused. Arthur was already awake and sitting a short distance from me, staring at me with something like concern. "Another dream?" he asked.

Dawn was alive with bird-chatter and strange animal calls signaling good night and good morning - a chorus of intentions muddled by abundance. My mind was clouded, murky. I sat up, exhausted in spite of having slept.

I could see that Arthur was well - no claw marks or broken bones or, for that matter, wounds of any kind - yet I still felt upset, guilty. The vision had felt entirely real and I had trouble reconciling the feeling of it with the reality before my eyes.

Arthur bit the stem of his pipe and drew deeply. He was whole and entirely unafraid. I felt a rush of relief and sighed heavily. Then, instinctively, I pressed my hands to my torso, searching for the wounds from the previous evening.

"Must have been some dream, boy," he said.

The dream played out again in my head, distant, disjointed. I only nodded absently, still struggling to shake off the emotional certainty of my terrible dream.

Arthur snorted.

"Yes," I said. "But this one was... different". "It felt..." I stopped short. I felt it but could not see it and did not have the words to communicate this to him. Moreover, I wasn't sure I wanted to share it all with Arthur just yet. Still, I struggled for words for my own sake. "It felt like..."

"Like a memory," he said.

I nodded in agreement.

"Hold on to it," he said solemnly. I could see he had more to say on the matter but he stopped there.

I swallowed once, my mouth suddenly dry.

Interlude: Instincts

It all happened, it seemed, in a single moment; Arthur had come upon him sleeping. He had taunted. And Shadrach, taken by the wildness he deemed made him unfit, now stood atop a corpse, panting, painted in bright blood.

He had lunged with full strength and eager fangs directly toward the old man's throat and had found more than a suitable purchase.

He bit deep and savored the rush of it, the hot copper scent of blood; even the horrible gore congealed and spread afterward - it all fed him. And, though the resultant spurting of blood,, made him feel as though this were not what he wanted and could not be, he found himself chatting, barking, howling. Yet, even with satisfaction red-raw in his mouth, even just moments after the deed, he felt no relief.

It had ended too quickly. Shadrach saw Arthur's sword lay upon the ground, feigning also to be a dead thing.

Before he was aware of why, Shadrach spat the blood from his mouth. It landed as a grey white mess upon the grass. He would understand later, remembering as the claws came for him, remembering the crunch and tearing he was made to do, the pale and needle-fingered cretins falling all around him; he would remember how they had tried with all of their might and yet had not touched him.

Now, though, he stepped into the well of himself and felt the hot tightening of his skin; he moved aside and was biting into another as the first slashed into the nothing where he once stood. And then another. And another.

It wasn't long before a pile began to form.

Later, he would recall that he could not recall exactly what he had done. He only knew that what had taken him was his wildness. And, in communion with his wildness, he had survived, and could not have without it.

Standing among the corpses, he felt himself, all at once, out of place. And, after examining himself, he found no wou-

"The boy."

Shadrach shot toward him with great haste, knowing.

Becoming

I felt that, if I really wanted, I could recall the whole thing. And, the more I thought of it, the more I was certain that I could. For the first time since waking, I felt something other than helplessness, confusion, or fear. I felt powerful - threatening, even.

I looked at the old man and he stood clumsily, nearly tripping over himself in the process. His fearful bungling made me feel even more alive. I smiled. I couldn't help it. I imagined him on his knees, begging me for his life, snotting, drooling, weeping like a child - the image filled me with something like joy, something like pure ecstasy. It was intoxicating. I stood and began walking toward him and felt it difficult not to begin smiling. He began to backpedal.

"Easy there, boy."

My teeth felt uncomfortable in my mouth, unruly, my hands began to itch furiously, my skin suddenly too tight, not my skin, not my hands, not my mouth. My body began to feel flimsy, trivial.

He continued to back away, never taking his eyes off of me. "Gentle there, pup. Settle down."

"I was beautiful once." The voice that came out of me was strange and familiar all at once. I felt my skin prickle with familiarity. I stretched my jaw and felt more teeth, larger teeth. I grabbed a nearby tree in my fist and felt the wood give way in my grasp.

"What, pray tell, do you reckon you hold in this boy-cage, beloved? A beast? Something to tame? To prop up for show, confined to a mock-existence, marooned behind half-lidded eyes. Did you think the boy-cage would render me docile and obedient?"

Arthur, still backing away, tried to draw his sword but tripped once again and fell flat on his back, knocking the wind out of him.

The old man cried out in terror and began backing away on his hands and feet. In an instant, I was upon him, my foot on his chest, still smiling. "I am God's hand, boldest son of the Elder Peaks. Do you remember, beloved? Oh, but you must."

"Peace, creature." I turned to see a large grey wolf standing a short distance away. It spoke again. "Do him no harm."

The fear-stink of the old man was overwhelming. Nevertheless, I turned my full attention to the wolf. There was no hurry. I could have them both if I wanted. I knew it.

"Do you remember me, beloved?" Arthur nodded. The wolf stiffened slightly but did not back down. "Yes"

"I shall leave you both open and rotting in a tree of my choosing. "

The wolf starred, motionless. "I beg you, creature, stay your hand."

"I shall have you both. Him, because I am hungry. But you - you I will have for sport."

I felt the sword pass through my middle smoothly and with no pain. I looked down to see the old man, now covered in blood, both hands pushing the sword into me up to the hilt. I grabbed his hands and the sword, pulling the blade out easily and crushing everything in my grasp. When my claws dug into his hand, he let loose a trembling howl.

I did not expect his sword to break so easily. It was satisfying. I had watched as he struck down my (Its) children. I had watched as they were torn, tortured, vanquished. The cost had been immense, much more than I (It) had expected. But, at last, iit was finished. At last, his blade of power was undone. And, now, It would not be interrupted in delivering Arthur to the same fate.

An unnatural calm came over us.

His blade falling asunder and to the earth, I looked down at him, eager to have my meal. But there was... a shift. An alteration. Was it him? Had he changed somehow? I looked into his face and saw no fear of death, only pain, his eyes shut tight against a mask of his blood. And, yet... the smell that surrounded him. I couldn't not discern its origin...

I heard the wolf begin to advance with great speed. Grinning, I turned to meet him.

Name and Purpose

This was not waking, but turning. At one moment, I turned. And there he was. And, there, the world was not. We were in some shadowed corner of Its mind, some nether realm in which he held court. It was strange, but not entirely unfamiliar.

I felt that I might have been here before. And then-

Ogmwa suenin rundetsun...

-at once, I knew where I was. Where we were. Perhaps recognizing my realization, It spoke, the voice cutting into me, seeming to wear at the few tethers that held me in place. In *this* place.

"You should have let me have you when I took you the first time. It would have been easier."

"Not a dream, but a memory," he had said. *"Hold on to it."*

"You seemed to have enjoyed the sweets," it called. Hearing it, even in mock pleasant tones, felt like a repetitive pain. And cold.

Hold on to It

I braced against it and dug in. "Who is... Danforth?"

It laughed, unconcerned. "You see more than most, but cannot see yourself. Look how easily I have turned you."

A veil was lifted, and I saw myself for the first time. I saw my body, now, this thing, this monster, savaging Arthur. It was a curious thing to see him on his knees. It had not occurred to me how completely I believed in him, in his power and ability to protect me, to follow through on his word.

But, seeing how I had changed and what had changed me, seeing the fullness of fear in his eyes, I realized that I had been here - watching from a distance -

for some time. And this thing I had become…

I thought back to Arthur's fingers down my throat and knew now that I hadn't understood.

"I dreamed that you would bring him to me. He could not evacuate me from you."

I thought of the stiffness in my midsection. The pinch. The-

"*suenin rundetsun*"

-incantation I had spoke from a place void of memory or knowledge. It came to me fully formed and pressed into words. I only opened my mouth and allowed it out.

"I did not dream that I would have you both - certainly not so easily."

Its voice tore through me like shards of ice. I braced myself against It, frozen and tearing. Still, remembering the lifted veil, I pressed into the vision it revealed.

I saw Arthur laying prone, his blade shattered like glass in my (Its) grasp. He had not been spared the sundering of the blade, a broken thing that rendered his hands a tangle of broken fingers and palms torn into pieces. He was bloodied. He was beaten. The wolf approached with urgency, and I (It) could feel in my (this) [that] body how easily It would and could catch him in my claws. And eagerly.

"You were starving," came the shards of Its voice. "So… enthusiastic."

I regretted then, withholding the dreams as I had. I regretted leaving the cage. The horror slowly began to consume me.

"He was clever, but not able," It taunted. "Look upon his clever hands! That sword! That monstrous knife that split apart my children, my warriors. My family."

The creature pressed further. "And now, as recompense, his weapon is as useful as that tangled batch of memories he calls Arthur."

Looking through the veil, I heard Arthur crying out in agony. My heart quickened.

"But you do not know... do you? No." The subtitles had fallen away. I could feel the thing in my brain. I knew then that he was taking both parts of me at once.

Hold on to It.

I held against the rabid insistence of my instincts.

"Arthur, son of Clifton - the memory merchant. Clever but not wise. Not wise enough. Not either of them."

I recalled the feeling of Arthur, whole and splintered, that I felt when he'd placed his hand upon my neck. I thought of all the fragments that weren't him, all of the pieces of memory with worn off faces.

"He stitched himself together," I pondered. "He filled in the missing spaces with... other people?"

I had just begun to grasp it, when, through the veil, I watched my claws extend. I could not watch him die, but could not call out to him; unless I could find a way to speak through my stolen body, he could not hear us.

"And now he is stitched together... by the very sword he used to sever-"

The creature halted abruptly and there was silence. Sensing his distraction, I dug in, this time mimicking Its subtly.

I thought I could also feel a... shift. Something had returned. Something was returned. I could not say. Whatever it was, Ogmwa had also become aware and it stole his focus. I could feel him contemplating, recognizing, until he had nearly forgotten me.

Arthur, now a silent ruin upon the ground, his eyes shut, was yet breathing. "His last breaths," It thought into my head.

"His name," I thought.

"The sword," It said, even now the sharpened misery of Its voice had less effect.

I felt It realize its fatal error too late. I watched, as It switched my (its) focus to Arthur, a moment too late.

Now trembling, his eyes flew open and he turned his face to the heavens, speaking aloud his true name.

The lightning fell, a crackling column of light descending from the sky to fall upon our heads. It slammed into the earth and cascaded outward, extending across the landscape in blinding undulations. Arthur rose from the ground, smouldering, smoke pouring from his mouth, His eyes bright and terrible.

The column consumed them all; the creature I'd become, the wolf that leapt to save me, and, at last, the man who'd called it down. He remained suspended in the air for a time, lightning emanating from him like spectral whips, arcing noisily. Then he fell to earth, charred and silent.

I saw myself, just a boy again. "Just a boy," I thought, as if hearing it from some other life.

I turned inward, and could feel that It was afraid of me.

"The lighting reached you too," I said. It was not a question. "How am I still here?"

I felt It struggle, the worm in my brain. Then, "This is only death."

Then nothing.

I was ejected from Its mind and sat up in my own body, breathing as if for the first time. I turned in time to see Arthur, scorched and singed, dragging himself toward the wolf. I stood and ran toward him, screaming.

I could see it.

He placed a hand upon the corpse of the wolf, and I watched as he was reformed before my eyes; every hair, every tooth, every claw. The wolf stood, reconstituted in full. Arthur lay still in the ashes.

I came upon them and caught Arthur by the hand. Even as this burned husk, he managed to close his hand around mine. There was no transfer nor jolt of memory this time. Only touch. Only us.

And the wolf.

I tightened my grip on Arthur's hand, suddenly aware of my loneliness and the nearness of the wolf. Arthur did not return the squeeze.

Rider

We collected his body, determined to bury him far from the mouth of Gana Brielle. But where?

Shadrach offered no clue.

We stood there, silent sentries over a corrupted body, mourning. And then... a flicker?

Careful now. Eyes closed. Gently. See him.

Though I knew he would not return it, I knelt down and squeezed his hand again, feeling I had to be sure, knowing I never would be.

The charred body lay inert, and I wept for the loss of knowing. And then. His hand. Before I was sure of it, his hand had begun slowly closing around mine. I felt the wholeness of him then, diminished, but present. I had too many questions and none of them mattered. I covered his hand in mine and sighed a shuddering breath.

"You deserved a better death than this," I said, fighting a quivering lip.

His eyes, his face, his entire body had been burned to the darkest char. I saw and heard him struggle to open his eyes and did not get the meaning.

"Lay still," I said gently. I sat down beside him and bowed my head as I looked upon him.

Despite my request, it seemed he would continue to try and open his eyes. "Lay still," I said once more. "Please."

There was a slight cracking sound as his right eye burst open. Looking into that bloodied eye, I felt him squeeze my hand a final time.

As we sat there, I remembered his great tangle of black and silver whiskers, his haunted hungry gaze, those black eyes set in an impassable face. The memory drew an unexpected gasp from my lips pressed together with the effort of concentration.

"Like a memory," he had said.

"Hold onto it," he had said.

Easy now. Breathe.

At first, it was as if I could smell him; a patchwork of grasses and flung hay, animal stink, a dank mixture of wood and, of course, smoke. I see him differently in this moment and press into the vision. I feel my hands slide into his like a glove, his fingers are my fingers. I feel his heart, now our heart, beating dutifully. A welcome breeze cuts the warmth of the late Spring sun and we shiver. We retrieve a fist full of dried lavender and jasmine from his pocket and hold it to our nose, our cheek, our chest, our nose - a modest liturgy to conjure a memory. Our eyes, dark, soft, distant, wander out past the horizon, beyond the stark Obligashi Mountains and the lush rolling green of the Bahn Meadow Valley, across the sweet wine dark waters of the Parshiquay River and, further still, beyond all we had traversed until our gaze settled on -

Home. At long last I am returned home to Ashmane. Oh how my heart has long ached for the smell of this land! And yet, having returned, how it now aches all the more. But it is a good pain. An honest pain. I am healing. I am home.

I run whooping and shouting through the whispering fields, abandoning my burdensome pack to the grasses, stripping my filthy clothes, leaving my sword to rust against a nameless tree. Running still, I splash into the river and submerge, heedless of the biting cold. The water rushes over my skin and into my open laughing mouth. I slap the surface and cry out to no one, blood thundering in my ears, sun glinting on my chest and arms, my sins and scars forgotten. I remember myself. I am home again.

Inside, I gorge myself on sweet cream and bread, my beard a tangled mess of crumbs and honey. I dress, and lay, for a while, on my bed, marveling at the softness, wondering if I might ever again become accustomed to such a luxury.

*Giddy still, I cross the wide field between the house and my workshop. I am
hectored all the while by the persistent grunt-snort-nuzzle of Celus, begging
for an apple, a carrot, some raisins, please. I empty my pockets, telling Celus
of the majesty of Westpeak, the child-thieves of DavStagom and the
whistle-clicking birds of the Elder Peaks who speak with the voices of men. I
show him my scars, pantomiming my battles, laughing aloud, snarling,
smacking his sides, enduring the rebuke of his playful bites. I feel the muzzle of
my marvelous and greedy horse against my chest and my heart quickens
again. I am home.*

*Our blood afire, we race across the field, gliding blade-smooth through the
grasses, charging up and over hills, whisper-rushing past trees and under
branches, faster still, through the ravine and into Jeb's meadow, blurring the
landscape with our frantic pace. There is only the next rise, bend, hill,
full-speed through the valley, turn, even faster now, my arms about his neck,
the pair of us, a fury of storming hooves and clenched fists, thrumming with a
single heart. The tears will not stop coming and I fear my heart will burst but
we run, he and I, off into forever.*

*In the evening, after a careful look over each shoulder, I wander into the small
wooden shed to retrieve my pipe, hidden in a wooden box beneath a false
plank near the northern wall. My treasure recovered, I carefully sat myself in
my favorite chair, opened the small box, and set about my ritual.*

*Taking the pipe in one hand, I carefully work a thin stick through the stem,
pausing occasionally to dump out a little here and there, gently blowing
through the pipe, expelling the old ash. Then, setting the pipe aside, I grab my
pouch, pushing one a finger into the top, stirring the pouch open, and, finally,
bringing the pouch to my face to bury my nose and grunt contentedly. I gently
pick apart any clumps in the tobacco, setting aside this bit and returning that
bit to the pouch. Then, I trickle strands of tobacco into the bowl of the pipe
until it is filled to the top, tamping it gently. Just before lighting it, I put the
pipe to my lips and draw once, twice, swaddling my tongue in phantom flavor,*

nodding with approval. Here I cast a final wary glance over his shoulder, perking up my ears a bit just to be sure that I am alone. Satisfied, I light the pipe, drawing deeply, expelling great blue-grey plumes of smoke. At first, the acrid smoke stings my eyes, forcing me to bark a cough or two. But soon, we are reacquainted, and the air is crowded with blue grey plumes and lazy smoke rings.

From just outside the door I hear (and pretend not to notice) a sneeze. I go about my business, closing my eyes, tasting the smoke, my heels resting on the table. The door creaks open the slightest bit and no more. I wait, drawing nonchalantly on my pipe, feigning ignorance. Yet, though I judged myself prepared, I am surprised when the aging door is thrust open. I am quick to my feet but not quickly enough. I am tackled to the ground, buffeted about the face and neck.

My attacker is tiny but relentless, slapping me and pulling hard at my beard. "Spare me!" I plead. "I am an old man!"; an entreaty met only with derisive laughter.

"SURRENDER!" my attacker shouted. "SURRENDER AND I MAY LET YOU LIVE!

Having had enough, I roll atop my assailant pinning him to the ground. As he squirms beneath me, I draw deeply from my pipe and spew a cloud of smoke into his mouth and eyes. He coughs and struggles, but does not relent.

"Had enough?" I jeer.

"NEVER!" he cries.

"Never?" I ask, putting my pipe between my teeth and tickling him. Now the struggle becomes outright flailing as he squeals helplessly, tears streaming from his eyes.

"NEVER!" he manages between chortling gasps. "NEVER!" In spite of the game, his voice was sure, strong, certain.

We laugh, and it is good to laugh.

In that instant, he flings his arms about my neck, now sobbing with relief. I stand, bringing my son with me, each of us overwhelmed with tears. He embraces me even tighter, pressing his cheek into my beard. I hold him close, then closer still, afraid that I might crush him yet unable to restrain myself. And I find myself unable to do much more than hold him as close as I'm able and weep with him.

"It's ok. I'm home now, son." I say, assuring him and myself. "I'm home."

Shadrach noticed the tears standing in my eyes.

"He meant to come home," I said aloud. "He always meant to come home. And he did."

I surrendered to the moment and wept. Then, gently clearing my throat, I replied, "I know where to bury him. I know where home is."

"It is a long way," Shadrach said meekly.

Arthur's eye remained open and wild, but the vision had ceased. His chest no longer rose and fell. I closed his eye and looked up toward Shadrach with a pleading gaze. Shadrach seemed to struggle a bit before settling on an answer.

"To Ashmane," he said. "And a proper burial."

Even weeping, I smiled. It was a relief, knowing. This was what he deserved. Then, after a moment of thought, I asked "Which way?"

Shadrach snorted and began moving East.

Drew John Ladd is an author/activist/public speaker living in East Haddam, Connecticut with his dogs, Friday and Jack. He enjoys gardening and tea (Earl Grey, hot). He also has a deep passion for American History, American Political Theory and holds a degree in Political Science from the University of Connecticut.

Ladd is also a passionate lifelong musician and has instructed a nationally competitive marching band for much of his adult life.

You can continue to discover and support what Ladd is currently working on at:

www.patreon.com/drewwritesstuff

He may also be found on **Facebook** and **Twitter**;

Facebook: https://www.facebook.com/drewjohnladd/

Twitter: https://twitter.com/drewwritesstuff

9 781716 120527

Made in the USA
Middletown, DE
03 May 2021